TEQUILA BLUES
BIJOU HUNTER

Cover
Photographer: NAS CREATIVES
Source: Shutterstock
Cover Copyright © 2017 Bijou Hunter

Dedication
Sally, Mike, Jack, Max, and Luca for loving me unconditionally
My bitching betas Debbie and Sarah
Judy's Proofreading

§

ONE — DAYTON

There aren't many things in my life that I'll lose sleep over. *My mom?* Sure. *My dad?* He's lived a good life. My brothers, Camden and Hudson, matter, but it's not like I spend much time thinking about them one way or another. I give a shit about my club. Having grown up in the Serrated Brotherhood Motorcycle Club, they're my second family. But they all got their own worries. They ain't losing sleep over me, and I can't say I lose much over them either.

The only person in this world that keeps me up at night is Harmony Tequila Slater. She isn't my girlfriend. We aren't even friends. More like acquaintances with benefits. I've known her for years, seen her grow up from a beautiful teenager to a stunning woman. Her sister, Daisy, recently married my twin brother, Camden. Her other sister is hooked up with my cousin, Bonn. So, I guess Harmony and I are family now. But that isn't why I care.

Harmony doesn't know she's my woman yet. If I had bigger balls and a smaller ego, we'd have settled shit long ago. She'd be in my bed every night, and her three-year-old son would have my blood running through his veins.

But I didn't do what needed to be done. Now, I'm losing sleep over her every night.

Tonight, though, when I find her enjoying a drink at the Red Barn Bar, I know the time's come to do what I should have done years ago.

This is the night when Harmony will learn she's mine.

TWO — HARMONY

For what feels like forever, I've had a crush on a bad man. Dayton Rutgers isn't misunderstood or simply complicated in a way normal men aren't. *He's the bad guy.*

Dayton drinks too much. Fucks any available woman. Says whatever he wants without worrying about feelings or consequences. He commits acts of violence for his motorcycle club and likely for fun.

Admittedly, he isn't all bad. I mean, Dayton's loyal to his family and club. But I know he can't be with his lovers. Women are disposable to him, yet most don't care. After all, he's so damn sexy. If the rumors are true, he's also talented in bed.

Over the years, I've heard the sex part secondhand from his many conquests. Hickory Creek Township is a small place where everyone knows everyone's business. Especially about the rich and beautiful people like Dayton and his wealthy, powerful family.

Though I've long dreamed of trying out Dayton's sexual talents up close and personal, I'm terrified of falling for a man with no love for anyone these days. *Even himself, apparently.*

Usually, I avoid Dayton. The exceptions are those two nights a month when I clear my head by enjoying a few fruity cocktails at the Red Barn Bar. No one bothers me here, not since Dayton and I made out in a back booth. That night, the booze and lust tempted me to indulge in more than flirting.

Around me tonight, people speak in hushed tones. The low, red lighting and bluesy music put everyone in a relaxed mood. Closing my eyes, I inhale the scent of beer, B.O., and way too much perfume.

"I'll have what she's having," Dayton says, suddenly appearing next to me at the bar top.

"It's a mango ginger fizz," I explain without looking at him. "You continue to surprise me, Dayton."

Sitting next to me at the bar top, he doesn't change his order even after realizing what it is.

I admire the rich scent of the hot night on his bare skin, only inches from my lips. He's a delicious man, and I crave his kisses. But they come with a price.

"Whatcha doing here alone?" he asks, leaning forward, so his shoulder-length blond hair frames his handsome face.

"You always ask me that when you find me alone. What did I say last time?"

"Go away, perv," he murmurs while wearing a smirk.

Fighting a grin, I nod. "Oh, yeah, well, before that."

"Your sisters won't drink in public."

Turning to him, I refuse to show him how much he affects me. "Are you planning to whine about your mommy and daddy again? If the answer is yes, keep in mind how I'm not in the mood."

"Hurts me real deep when you use that tone," he says, snatching my hand from the bar top. "Have you been crying?"

"Do you really care?"

"Why do you have to be so mean?"

Studying his expression, I pull away my hand and focus on my drink. "My client died."

Dayton opens his mouth. I brace myself to hear something shitty that'll inspire me to hate him.

He might sense he's heading down a bad road because he asks, "I'm sorry. Did she suffer?"

Smiling at how he can say the right thing when he wants, I sip my drink. "No, she went in her sleep."

"Is that code for during sex?"

Rolling my eyes, I smile. "That's the Dayton I know."

"What happens now?"

"I drink my drink, and we make small talk, and then I leave."

"I mean, with your job now that your client died."

3

I don't answer immediately, taken aback by his ability to give a crap. Dayton downs his fizz in two gulps and orders a beer.

"The company I work for has found another house for me," I finally explain. "This one is home to three autistic women around my age. I met them yesterday."

"Do you like them?"

"Difficult to tell since they have autism and don't warm up to people off the bat. I hope in a few weeks they'll trust me, and I'll see more of their personalities."

"Huh? Your job takes brains," he says, tapping my forehead. "I thought it only involved cleaning up puke and wiping asses."

"It does, but not all asses are the same."

"No, they're not."

Holding his gaze, I sip my drink until I've nearly finished it. "What are you thinking?"

"That you're too beautiful for me not to have fucked yet."

"Yeah, I figured it was something romantic like that."

My disinterested tone is completely betrayed by the shiver I feel at him speaking so bluntly of what we've only teased at for so long.

"We're family now," he says in a low, seductive voice. "Through marriage and all. Seems like we ought to stop dancing around the inevitable."

"I'm not drunk enough to say yes to that line of thinking."

"Then, I'll order you another drink, and we'll see where things go."

Smiling, I let him buy me another fizz. When he leans forward to plant a soft, wet kiss on my neck, I struggle to keep my panties from dropping to the floor that very second.

His gaze holds mine as we wait for my drink.

"How's your kid?" he asks.

"Why do you care?"

"Anything connected to you matters to me."

"Oh, it does?"

4

Dayton leans forward again. This time his lips don't find my throat. They instead land squarely on my waiting lips. The noise in the bar fades away, and I'm alone with Dayton's skillful tongue.

"You taste good," I murmur once he frees my lips.

"It's the mango ginger crap."

I reach for my new drink with one hand and wrap a lock of his hair around the finger of my other.

"Want to go to the booth?"

"Only if this time we start there and end in my bed."

"No, not your bed. I can't have Daisy knowing my dirty secrets. Well, at least not until I've edited out the worst parts."

"Then, your bed. I'm assuming your little man is with Grandma."

"We'll see," I say, sliding off the barstool.

"See what?"

"If you can make me want you so badly that my common sense turns off for long enough to say yes."

Dayton smirks, clearly accepting my challenge. I love how his dark eyes sparkle with mischief. He's the only man I've ever craved or feared. But tonight, my defenses are down, and my hunger runs hot. I'm tempted to stop dreaming and give in to the fantasies we've nursed for too long.

THREE — DAYTON

Harmony giggles when drunk, and she's giggling something fierce right now. My lips leave the soft flesh of her throat long enough for me to frown at her amused face. Her pale green eyes shine with humor while she swings back her long blonde ponytail. I swear she's reacting to a joke no one else can hear. *Apparently, those fizzes make her nuts.*

"Do you want me to stop?" I ask before my lips immediately return to her throat.

"You were right about my baby staying with his grandma tonight," she says, stroking my cock through my blue jeans. "That means my trailer is empty. Want to finally see if you and I have as much fun naked as we do with our clothes on?"

"Did you just ask me to fuck you?" I whisper in a ragged voice.

Harmony licks her lips. "Are you sober enough to drive because I'm not?"

"I don't care if I have to walk to your place with you hanging off my shoulder. I will get us there and make you spread."

Sliding out of the booth, Harmony smiles at me. "You won't have to make me do anything." When I join her, she adds, "I don't even think we need to worry about foreplay. I'm that wet right now."

My gaze flashes to where her pussy hides behind a pale pink skirt. Returning my attention to her face, I wouldn't mind getting her spread eagle on the table and doing her right here. Of course, then I'd need to kill everyone in the bar to prevent them from knowing what my woman looks like naked. *Yeah, probably easier to take her back to the trailer.*

Harmony is sober enough to remain on the Harley until we arrive at a gas station, where she nearly topples on her ass. I steady the giggling blonde who won't stop grabbing for my dick.

6

"I need to pick up protection."

"Oh, but I have a giant box of condoms at my place," she says, laughing again.

"Don't hurt yourself while I run inside."

Harmony gives me a thumbs-up and dances around to the music playing from the station's overhead system. I run into the store to buy a box of condoms. In the past, I always kept them handy. I still have some at my condo, but that's not where we're headed.

Returning quickly, I discover Harmony flipping off passing cars.

"What are you doing?"

"I'm a rebel sticking it to society," she explains and then wraps her hand around the back of my neck and yanks me down to kiss her.

As sweet as she tastes, I know we need to stop kissing and get to her trailer before my dick tears free from my frayed jeans.

"Hold on," I say, picking up Harmony and setting her on the Harley.

Wrapping her arms around my waist, she tightens her grip enough for me not to worry about her toppling off during the two-minute ride to her place. Once at the Lush Gardens Trailer Park, I pry her fingers loose from my shirt she's fisted during the ride.

The moment I haul Harmony off the bike, she slides under my baggy white T-shirt and licks my left nipple.

"Talk about a horny devil," I say, peering down at her from the collar.

A flushed-faced Harmony smiles at me. "I'm drunk and horny. Yet, you're wasting this fabulous opportunity to defile me, Dayton Rutgers. I should add my vibrator wouldn't be so ungrateful."

Removing her from my shirt, I lift her off the ground and carry her princess-style toward her trailer. She wraps her arms around my neck and kisses my throat before settling on nibbling at my ear.

"Don't pass out," I mutter, terrified she'll stick me with a severe case of blue balls while she naps for the rest of the night.

"I haven't fucked anyone in so long," she whispers. "I wonder if I'll remember how."

Harmony proves her rusty moves once we're inside her dark trailer. Her shirt gets caught on her head, forcing me to stop messing with the condoms long enough to save her. She then topples on the bed while removing her shoes. Most memorably, she jumps when I touch her pussy, and her knee makes a beeline for my balls.

Somehow, I pin down her wayward limbs long enough to slide on a condom and shove my dick inside her.

Romance out the window, we fuck like animals for an hour. I'm too drunk to do much more than pump wildly into her body and enjoy her pussy after so long fantasizing about it. Harmony is so drunk that she doesn't accomplish much more than coming hard and say my name. *At least, she knows I'm the guy plowing her in the dark room.*

We fuck until she passes out after patting my head and claiming I should go pro. Surrounded by wood-paneled walls, I watch Harmony for nearly a half-hour before cuddling next to her damp body. Her trailer's overheated, and I'm sweaty from fucking Harmony into submission. I'd kill for a fan to cool me down, but I don't dare leave the bed and wake her. No, I've waited too damn long to have Harmony Tequila Slater asleep against me with my arms wrapped protectively around her soft body.

Tonight, I took the first step by working my way into her bed. Now, I just need to figure out how to stay in her life.

FOUR — HARMONY

The morning after I take the drunken leap with my long-time crush, I wake up with a mild hangover, a screaming vagina, and a gorgeously passed-out Dayton. The hunk of a man looks out of place in my bed, as if a movie star stepped off the silver screen and into an episode of "Hoarders." No doubt, I should schedule a time to de-clutter my room, but that's a worry for another day.

Dayton's blond hair partly covers his handsome face, but the rest of him is perfectly naked. I gently change positions so I can better admire his hard curves. I notice a hickey on his chest, just above his right nipple. Did I give it to him? Or was it from one of the many women who've called Dayton their lover?

Finally sliding out of bed, I'm relieved to see my wastebasket full of condoms. I don't doubt Dayton gets regular check-ups to ensure his dick doesn't decay from disease. On the other hand, the first time I had sex, I got pregnant. No way do I want my second experience to end with an STI.

I turn on the shower and let it run. While waiting for the hot water to kick in, I make a pot of coffee and check my phone for messages.

My baby, Keanu, sent me a photo of himself before going to bed at Grandma Sally's. He smiles big for the camera, always getting a little too close. I grin at the sight of his sweet face.

Once the water gets hot, I take a quick shower, washing away the festivities from last night. I keep expecting Dayton to wake up from the noise, but he's still sprawled out on my bed when I return to the room to find clothes.

Deciding to wake him, I try a few different tactics. A cup of coffee near his face does nothing. I say his name more than once and bounce on the bed, but the man remains dead to the world.

I check the clock and realize I need to walk over to my mom's trailer to pick up Keanu soon. As sexy as Dayton looks in my bed, he needs to get up... NOW!

I take a wet cloth and rub it against his face. When that doesn't work, I sprinkle the cold water on his balls. Again, Dayton refuses to wake up.

Drenching the cloth in cold water, I drop it on his crotch. *Yeah, that did it.*

"What the fuck?" he yells, taking a swing at me.

I dodge his lame strike, much like I do with my rowdier clients. Dayton looks around the room before his dark-eyed gaze focuses on me.

"We fucked last night," he says in case I missed this tidbit.

"Are you sure?"

Ignoring his frown, I grab the cloth and notice his dick harden.

"No," I say, backing away. "You need to get dressed."

"I'm tired as hell. What time is it?"

"Nearly nine. I need to get my boy, so you need to get going."

Dayton throws his long legs over the side of the bed and forces his massive body to sit up. I avoid noticing his dick and how the damn thing keeps expanding until I'm unsure it'll fit into his pants.

"Here's coffee. If you need a quick shower, have at it. But I need you to light a fire under your sexy ass. Okay?"

Dayton sips the coffee, watching me with sleepy eyes. "You like my ass, huh?"

"That's why I brought you back here last night."

Dayton smiles. "You ran the show, did you?"

I kneel in front of him and exhale softly. "We both knew this would eventually happen. Though I'm glad it did, you can't stay here."

"Not ready to make it official, huh?"

"What?"

"Us."

"We're not... Look, just get dressed and go before I'm forced to drag you out."

10

"Think you could?"

"I move full-grown adults for work. I think I could handle you, too."

"Bullshit. I'm twice your weight."

"Fine," I say, standing up. "I'll yank you by the hair and tug your stubborn ass out of my house. Why ruin a fun night by making me manhandle you?"

Dayton sips the coffee again before setting the cup on the side table. He takes his jeans I hand him.

"I don't know where your underwear ended up."

"Didn't wear any. I guess I knew I'd be in a rush."

"Charming. Now get out."

Laughing, Dayton stands up and cups my jaw. "You are not a morning person, huh?"

"I need to get Keanu."

"The kid can wait a little," he says, running his fingers down my jaw to my throat and likely heading south.

"No, he can't. He's three, and he's waiting for his mom to pick him up so we can spend our day together."

Dayton keeps his mouth shut while shoving his feet in the boots I located in the living room. Once he's dressed, his gaze locks on me. Sighing, I know my struggles are far from over.

"When are we hooking up again?" he asks, coming toward me.

I back out of the room and head for the door. "Whenever we see each other at the Red Barn again, I guess."

"You only go a couple of times a month. That ain't gonna work. Let me take you out for dinner."

Shaking my head, I reach for the handle, but his hand quickly covers mine.

"A drink then," he says in the kind of voice people don't refuse.

I stare into his sexy eyes and smile at how I've finally enjoyed Dayton Rutgers's talents. "Fine. We'll have a drink in a few weeks."

"Tonight."

"I don't drink on Sundays."

11

"Then Monday."

"I work Mondays."

"Tuesday."

Seeing where this is headed, I sigh. "We can go out on Friday."

Dayton considers my offer before nodding. "Where's my kiss goodbye?" I pucker up for a quickie, but he shakes his head. "I made you come a lot last night. I want a good kiss full of your sweet tequila."

"Always with the tequila crap," I grumble and grab his shirt to tug him down to me.

Even sporting morning breath, Dayton tastes addictive. In a different world, I'd ask him to hang around. We could go out to breakfast with Keanu, and I'd see how they got along.

Except I know how Dayton will behave around my kid. He's never once used Keanu's name. I have no doubt he'd say something rude or scary. Then I'd get angry, and Dayton would be absolutely shocked to learn he did anything wrong.

So as much as I crave this handsome stud, I can't forget who and what he is. Dayton Rutgers is a bad man, and he puts himself first with everyone every time. No drunken night of passion can change who he is at his core.

FIVE — DAYTON

When Harmony kicks me out of her trailer, I walk square into Camden and Bonn along with their women. My brother gives me his usual grief, but I'm not in the mood. I'm hungover, and my erect dick rages at being shoved into my tight jeans instead of Harmony's snatch.

Driving to my condo building where Camden and Bonn also live, I'm relieved to know they aren't around to bother me. I plan to sleep for ten hours and wake up only once the sun is low in the sky.

I'm not a daytime person. The shades in my two-bedroom condo are always down, and I rarely get up before five in the evening. That's been my life for a long fucking time. But I know changes are coming.

Stripping out of my clothes, I crawl into bed and yank a sheet over my sweaty body. Harmony's trailer was a sauna. My condo's air conditioning quickly cools my hot flesh. I close my eyes and think about how Harmony laughed when drunk and how serious she was this morning. Only a special kind of woman could be that beautiful no matter her mood.

I dream of crashing my Harley and ending up in the hospital, where Harmony is my doctor. She's cold and won't give me pain meds. When I call her a bitch, she turns off my life support.

Waking up, I consider my dream a win. *After all, Harmony made a really fucking sexy doctor.*

The clock reads three, and I can't figure out why I'd wake up so early. Resting my head back on the pillow, I finally notice the knocking at my front door.

Twenty minutes later, the person is back at it. There are only a few people capable of annoying me this much.

Stumbling into a pair of boxers, I make my way to the door and open it to find Camden on the other side.

"Finally got into Harmony's pants, huh?" he says, pushing past me. "I was beginning to think you were only

13

faking your interest in her. Why else would it take so damn long to make the sale?"

He finishes babbling before I shut the door. Half asleep, I shuffle into the kitchen and look for a beer. Coffee would be better, but I rarely have anything to eat or drink at my place. In fact, there isn't even a single beer in my fridge.

Lowering my mouth under the faucet, I drink water before splashing some on my face to wake up.

"I came by earlier, but you wouldn't answer. Went to hang with Daisy, who sent me back. She wants details."

"I don't know what you're talking about," I say, leaning against the countertop. "Do you have coffee at your place?"

"Of course. Married life means a fridge full of food and an always perking pot of coffee. Wanna come over?"

"Not if it means I'll get interrogated about something that's none of your fucking business."

"Bad night, huh?" he says, grinning. "Harmony did seem pretty disappointed this morning."

Staring at my obnoxious brother, I unleash my angriest glare. He stares unimpressed back at me, and I admit he's a handsome motherfucker. Thick blond hair, rich brown eyes, a strong jaw—the guy is a real fucking looker.

"I'm not telling you a damn thing," I finally say.

"At least give me a hint about the future. Like, will we have double dates with the Slater sisters? Or will we endure awkward family functions where Harmony dodges you?"

"Not saying a fucking thing."

Camden grins, but I can tell he's disappointed. When he hooked up with his woman, the world learned his every emotion. Their love demanded to be shouted from the rooftops. *He's such a drama queen that way.*

Even unsure how Harmony sees our future, I'm certain the way everything between us will end. How we get there is the fun part.

Not that I'll tell Camden any of this. He'll gossip to not only Daisy but our mom and probably our dad and no doubt to a dozen club guys. Shit, he'll probably drop by the beauty shop to ensure my news spreads far and wide.

SIX — HARMONY

As the youngest of three girls, most of my clothes were hand-me-downs. I was never the first at anything. Mom was almost too relaxed by the time I came along.

It wasn't all bad growing up as the family's baby. I was never alone, and my big sisters always watched out for me. Best of all, I knew my place in the world.

As the oldest, exotic Ruby is our leader. The middle child, silly Daisy, was our goofball. Being the youngest, I got to be the free-spirit who learned from her sisters' mistakes and knew I'd always have support when I messed up.

When people saw the three of us walking together, they understood our team dynamics if something went down. Ruby would punch you. Daisy would cry if you didn't stay down. I would run home and rat you out to Mom and her friends. Then, they'd show up with weapons to kick your ass. *We had a system.*

Now, my sisters are gone, having left Lush Gardens to live with their men in a fancy condo building on the other side of Hickory Creek Township. I don't blame them for wanting more. Yet, it's depressing to come home to see their empty trailers. Or, in Daisy's case, a trailer inhabited by a new cat lady.

On Saturdays, we still get together for karaoke night. Ruby leaves her eight-year-old daughter, Chevelle, at home with Bonn while Daisy ditches her three cats with Camden. After they moved out, I kept the karaoke machine as an unspoken promise that our girls' nights would never end.

Tonight, with Keanu at Sally's trailer for the evening, I make peach mojitos. Nearby, Daisy sings "Total Eclipse of the Heart" while swinging her dark-haired ponytail to the music. Ruby sits on the couch with a bowl of popcorn. She occasionally tosses a handful whenever Daisy hits a high note.

15

"Camden says I sing like an angel," Daisy announces once the song's over.

Ruby laughs. "A man will say anything to get sex."

"He doesn't need to lie for me to put out. I haven't gotten bored of it yet."

Wrapping her long, brown hair in a bun on her head, Ruby rolls her eyes. "Once you pump out a few kids, you'll put a 'Do Not Disturb' sign on your vagina. Sex will be reserved for anniversaries and birthdays."

"Camden is too sexy for that to happen."

Ruby can't resist teasing Daisy once she has her on the ropes. "He might get ugly when he ages."

"Nope," Daisy says immediately, refusing to lose the argument. "His parents are both keeping it tight. Cam will be fine."

After handing them their drinks, I take a deep breath and say the words, "I am ready to speak of the night I spent with Dayton."

My sisters stop bugging each other and stare at me. They don't ask questions. Don't even seem to breathe. I don't blame them for fearing I might clam up. This isn't the first time I've made this announcement since the morning they caught Dayton leaving my trailer.

"I drank three ginger fizzes and decided to see if he was as good in reality as in my fantasies."

"Was he?" Daisy whispers, eyes wide.

A shrug is my only answer. My sisters wait to see if I'll offer more details. When I don't, Ruby stands up and takes the microphone to sing her song.

My silence comes from being unsure of how I feel about Dayton. He's been my ideal fling for years. Back when I was in high school, I'd see him riding his Harley and get a whole lot of sexy ideas about him and me hooking up.

Then, I grew up and wondered how I'd feel about being a one-night stand. Dayton paid attention to me at parties and whenever he saw me around town. Once he got laid and the chase was over, he'd lose interest, and I wasn't ready to be dismissed.

So, I waited.

16

There were so many times I considered taking the plunge with him. Before I got pregnant with Keanu, we were flirting. I asked Dayton if he wanted to take me somewhere. He said yes, of course. I asked if he could promise not to treat me differently after spending the night together. Rather than giving any reassurances or even lying, Dayton froze up.

I still remember the look on his face that night at Tad Cline's party. It was somewhere between terror and lust. Rather than answer, Dayton said he forgot he needed to do something and bailed.

After that night—and having a baby—I never flirted with any intention of putting out. Dayton kept chasing as if the party freak out never happened. We built a solid routine for years.

Now, I've broken it and taken the plunge. *No promises required.* Not now that I'm a mom rather than an eighteen-year-old girl swooning over the sexy bad boy.

"I think I hoped Dayton was complicated," I say more to myself than to my sisters.

Ruby stops singing and turns off the music. I stare at the mojito in my hand and think about my expectations. *Why would I waste time with a man like Dayton?*

"I know he's not complicated. There are no hidden layers underneath his womanizing asshole exterior. I know that, but I think a part of me naïvely hoped he was more."

"Did he do something?" Daisy asks in a hushed tone.

"It's not what he did or didn't do. It's that he's Dayton Rutgers, and he's spent years flirting with me like I'm special. But I'm not. He's fucked everything in town. He wasn't spending his nights thinking about me. He's not that guy, so dating him won't lead to what I think deep inside I want."

"You never know," Daisy says. "I mean, who would have thought I'd end up with Camden?"

"Camden's the more down-to-earth twin."

"Is he, though?" Ruby asks. "He was a pig until one day he wasn't. Who's to say Dayton couldn't be the same way?"

"Are you saying that because you want me to end up with Dayton and move into the condo building and live down the hall from you?"

My sisters nod in unison. "It would be ideal," Ruby says.

Daisy smiles wider. "Then, we'll get Mom, Betty, Charlie, and Billy to move to the condo building, and the entire gang would be back together."

"Can you imagine Dayton with Keanu?" I ask, fighting a bad mood. "Can you imagine him with any kid?"

"He's sweet with Chevelle," Ruby says. "In fact, since we moved to the condo, he wears pants in the hallway instead of walking around in his boxers. The man is capable of change."

Sipping my drink, I sigh. "I fantasized about him for too long. Dayton can never compete with the man I've built him up to be in my head."

"Did Dayton ask to see you again?"

"He wanted to get a drink last night, but I bailed."

"A drink couldn't hurt," Ruby says, walking over to wrap an arm around my shoulders. "Just see how he is now that you've put out. Isn't it better to try than to always wonder what if?"

"Yeah, that's what you'd tell us to do," Daisy adds, joining us on the couch. "Now, you need to be fearless."

"You've survived disappointment before."

"I have," I mumble, allowing a grin. "I'm very resilient."

Ruby pats my hand. "You told me if I didn't give Bonn a chance, I'd never be able to move on even if he and I didn't work out. Now, take your own advice and get Dayton out of your system."

Despite their pep talk, I remain afraid. Am I really ready to ruin my fantasies with a painful reality check?

SEVEN — DAYTON

Adam "Mojo" Rutgers is an impressive guy. Big, scary, charming, smart, he's a man's man that women lose their panties for. I have a helluva lot of respect for my father and club president.

That doesn't mean I don't think he's past his prime and needs to get the fuck out of the way so Camden can take over.

I don't share this information with anyone because I don't believe in sharing information, period. People talk too much, giving away all their secrets.

Case in point, Camden is way too fucking chatty for my taste. He might look like me on the outside, but his brain is wired completely differently. Camden thinks like a leader and struts like he's already running the show. *Except he isn't running shit.* Worse still, the good-looking bastard hasn't noticed the giant target on his handsome back.

Mojo asks Camden and me to meet him at one of the club's side businesses. The bar is a dump and caters to the nastiest drunks in town. Right now, it's empty, allowing us to speak openly about the club's recent problems.

"Howler's on edge," Mojo announces immediately.

My uncle, Howler, grew up pampered as the only son of the wealthy Hallstead family. As a young man, he built the Serrated Brotherhood Motorcycle Club with my dad. Already living the easy life, now he has the power of the club at his back. To say Howler was a spoiled fucker would be an understatement.

"What's new?" Camden replies, immediately losing his good mood.

"He wants to go to war with Hayes over Common Bend."

"We all want shit," I say, setting my feet on the bar top and resting back in a chair.

Camden watches me, likely thinking I'll tip over. The guy loves physical humor. If I fall, he'll laugh until his woman is forced to change his diapers.

"I need you to take this seriously," Mojo growls in a mean-as-fuck voice that would scare me more if he weren't my daddy. "Can you do that just once, Dayton?"

"I take everything seriously. I'm sorry if my lack of tears and girlish panic makes you think otherwise."

My father stares at me with his dark eyes. As a kid, I liked how they shined when he was happy and how they hid his anger when he was pissed. Unlike my uncle, Mojo believes in hiding his worst qualities. Only those who know him best understand how awful he can be.

"JJ wants to get patched into the club, and Howler expects his boy to be fast-tracked."

I think about my newest bastard cousin. This one showed up months ago for a reunion with his deadbeat dad, Howler. For whatever reason, my uncle actually gave a shit. Now, JJ is getting fast-tracked into a club where normal guys take years to earn their patch.

"Like I said, we all want shit that won't happen," I mutter.

"Howler expects you two to put JJ through the wringer. But do it quickly, so he'll get his patch by the end of the summer."

Pulling out his super pissed but totally handsome frown, Camden nearly hisses, "Or we take our fucking time and see if we can push the fucker to leave."

"JJ won't go."

"You never know," I say, leaning farther back and giving Camden more hope that I'll fall. "JJ wants what he'll never get."

Dad asks, "What's that?"

"I'll let you know when he figures it out. The guy is a fucking headcase."

"I don't want him in the club," Camden states as if he's the one calling the shots.

Our father notices Camden's tone, too. They share a dark-eyed glaring match until I nearly tip over. Steadying myself, I smile at Camden.

"So close, but nope."

"Next time," he says, smirking.

"Look, here's what I think," I announce like I give a shit. "Now, I'm not the club president, and I never will be. No, I'm just a handsome sonovabitch who JJ considers his best buddy. So, what do I know anyway?"

"Just spill it," Dad says, rolling his eyes.

"JJ isn't a team player, and he certain as shit doesn't believe in loyalty. Not even to the mom he ditched, so he could come here and play nice with his long-lost daddy. A man who doesn't believe in loyalty has no place in the club."

"Then, he doesn't get in," Camden instantly says.

"That's not your call," Mojo reminds him. "Any member can sponsor a recruit. That doesn't mean he'll get a patch, but we've got to go through the motions."

"A waste of fucking time."

Camden is too busy thinking about his future as president. Mojo is focused on explaining to Howler that JJ failed to get a patch. Meanwhile, they miss the real threat.

Howler's a man past his prime who has everything to lose. JJ is a nobody wanting something he thinks we'll give him. When Howler lets JJ down, only a fucking idiot would expect the asshole to walk away peacefully. More likely, he'll burn down everything from the club to the town.

Dad claps his hands together to signal that he's made up his mind. "JJ will need to jump through the same hoops as everyone else."

"We jumped through them. Why the fuck shouldn't he?" Camden grumbles.

"We've buried two members in the last year," I remind them. "After the last one, it was Howler who freaked out about everyone wanting their every family member patched in. If I remember right, he said we're not running a book club. Also, we ought to have some fucking standards. You might want to remind him of that when he complains about us slow tracking JJ."

21

"Thanks, son," Mojo says, giving me a dirty look.

"You're welcome. I'm always here to lend a helping hand when you two get in over your fat heads."

"You and I have the same sized head," Camden says.

"Yeah, but I wear it better. Now, are we done hyperventilating, or is there more whining to do?"

"You in a hurry to get somewhere?" Mojo asks, cocking an eyebrow.

"I wanted to stop by Mom's place and eat pie."

"While you're there, ask if the Hallstead sisters have made their point, or do my balls need to remain in a vise?"

Trying not to laugh at his expression, I shake my head. "Yeah, I'm not asking that."

"Why the fuck not?"

"If she gets mad, I might not get pie."

"Then, ask after you get your fucking pie."

"Well, that'd just be rude."

Mojo looks to Camden for help, but he only shrugs. "It's good pie."

"I occasionally feel as if I did a shitty job raising you two."

"We occasionally feel that way, too," I say, leaning back in a chair again. "We're not going to war with Hayes, are we? I can't imagine it'd be fun to fight Bonn."

"He signed up to fight us. No pity." When Camden and I share an uncertain look, Mojo adds, "Bonn chose his side."

Camden narrows his handsome gaze. "Kinda seems like if your VP was the sort of man to treat his kids with a tiny bit of consideration, then maybe Bonn would have sided with us. Hell, maybe he could have convinced the Reapers to sell Common Bend to us instead of Hayes. But, no, Howler needed to be a dick father."

"Well, just until JJ came along," I point out.

"Yeah, I get it," Dad says, scratching at his jaw. "Howler is a shithead, but he's also your VP. You'll show the man respect."

"Consider it done," I say, leaning back farther and drawing Camden's attention.

Mojo rolls his eyes again. "You two are spoiled bitches."

"We get that from our paternal side of the family," I mumble while my chair nearly tips backward before I steady myself.

Camden grins. "It'll happen sooner or later."

Sharing my brother's smile, I look to Dad. "About Common Bend, you said what Howler wants. What about you?"

Mojo's right hand goes through his still thick hair. I know he always had his heart set on taking Common Bend from the Reapers. Now, he'd need to go through Hayes and Bonn. A war for Common Bend isn't what the Hallstead family wants. It's not what the club needs. Mojo knows all this, but he's a man accustomed to getting his way.

"Right now, we'll worry about JJ and how to get your mother and the Hallsteads under control. Once they're dealt with, we can consider Common Bend."

Though I don't react to his plan, Camden is clearly pissed. My brother wants to expand south toward Nashville. He envisions a future where we have chapters of the Brotherhood throughout the state. None of his big plans involve Common Bend. In fact, with our cousin now calling the shots there, Camden is more than happy to leave it alone.

But my brother isn't the club president, no matter how much he likes to pretend. He can't decide what the Brotherhood does or where it expands. I know Camden and how he wants to force Mojo and Howler to step aside. If he makes that move, I'll have his back.

So far, though, his balls haven't gotten big enough to force our father and uncle into retirement.

EIGHT — HARMONY

Taking my sisters' advice, I call Dayton and agree to have a drink with him the next Friday. He tries to push up the day, but I tell him it's Friday or nothing. For nearly a minute, Dayton's silent on the line. I suspect I've pissed him off. *Will he answer right now the question of our future together by ending things before they start?*

Dayton doesn't bail on our Friday plans. Instead, he makes a single request before hanging up. "Wear jeans on our date. That way, you can ride my Harley easier. Also, I won't be tempted to yank up your skirt and get busy in front of everyone."

When Dayton picks me up on Friday, I'm wearing the requested jeans along with a Duran Duran T-shirt. He struts up to my door with a sly smile on his face, and I can't help grinning back at him.

"You look happy."

"I knew you'd give in," he says, standing over me in the hot evening. "Knew you couldn't resist getting another taste."

Dayton leans down and covers my mouth with his. The arrogant jerk isn't wrong about how much I crave his flavor. For nearly two weeks, I've been thinking about his hands on me. *His body on top of mine. Him inside me.* Our night together made me a woman in a way my first time with sex didn't.

Tonight, we only share a kiss. Yet, I'm craving more, even if I know I shouldn't let my hormones call the shots.

Holding my hand, Dayton makes small talk while we head to his Harley. He asks about Keanu without using my son's name. Even mentions my new job before struggling to feel me up when helping me onto his bike.

I love the feel of the wind on my skin as we ride to the Brotherhood's bar, Salty Peanuts. My fingers grip Dayton's black T-shirt, soaking in the heat from his body. By the time

24

we arrive, I wish we stayed back at my trailer, where nudity would be more appropriate.

"It's packed tonight," Dayton says while helping me off his Harley. "Stay close."

Salty Peanuts' overhead speakers blast Ted Nugent in the parking lot, and the music is only louder once we're inside the bar. Unlike the Red Barn, this place is a full-stop honky-tonk. I'm overwhelmed by the heat of so many people packed together. The mix of cologne and perfume makes me gag, but I keep my mind on enjoying a night with Dayton.

Near the bar stand Mojo Rutgers and Howler Hallstead. They're whooping it up with a few other club guys I recognize. In fact, I probably "know" most of the people in Salty Peanuts, even if I've never met them. Hickory Creek Township isn't a big place and gossip rules.

Standing with Camden's cousin is a girl I haven't said two words to since high school. Bryana Baker was in the same grade as me, but we didn't know each other well. I kept to myself, especially after Daisy graduated.

Bryana wasn't popular, but she was stuck-up. Her family had a little money, and she was in the gifted classes, so she viewed herself as better than the rest of us. That's why I'm so surprised to see her at Salty Peanuts, wearing too much makeup and too few clothes.

I don't plan to acknowledge her. Since school, I've seen her a few times—grocery store, doctor's office, Taco Bell— and we did a fine job pretending to be complete strangers. Now, she's gyrating so hard against JJ, their beers spill on the floor.

"Let's leave," I say, stopping on a dime.

Dayton looks around, confused about why I'm no longer next to him. Turning around, he grunts. "What's the deal?"

"I want to leave."

"If it's the stink, I can get someone to spray air freshener. Do you like a clean linen scent?" he asks, smirking.

"It's not the smell, and an air freshener wouldn't defeat all this B.O. anyway. I just don't want to be here."

"Did I miss the part where you missed the part where I said we were coming here?"

"Do you see the woman using JJ as a vagina wipe?"

Dayton glances over his shoulder at his cousin and Bryana. "Do you mean the pink-haired lady having a seizure?"

Fighting a grin, I nod. "I knew her in high school, but we weren't friends. I don't want to have to pretend we are now, just because we're both, you know?"

"What?"

"Rubbing our vaginas on bikers."

"I think she's doing more than that with JJ."

I poke him in the chest, my finger meeting rock-hard muscle. "I'm doing more than that with you."

"I know you are," Dayton murmurs, giving me one of his smart-ass smiles.

"Can we just leave?"

"Nope. I want to talk to the piece of shit you're avoiding."

Before I can beg him to grow up, Dayton walks straight for JJ and Bryana. I consider remaining at the door. Then, a guy with a forehead tattoo comes within a few inches of me and smiles. I know he'll end up as a puddle on the ground if Dayton notices. This idiot has enough problems with his stupid sword-in-the-stone tat.

Hurrying over to Dayton, I hear him ask Bryana if she used to be a stripper.

"You look familiar, is all," he says when she tells him no.

"Harmony, right?" JJ asks, running his bony hand through his blond hair. "This is Bryana."

"Yeah, we went to high school together," I say, nodding at her.

"Yeah."

"How come you weren't BFFs?" Dayton asks, wrapping an arm around my shoulders. "Two pretty girls ought to be the best of friends."

I frown up at him, still hoping to avoid drama while he's dying to start crap.

26

"I was in the gifted classes," Bryana says. "She wasn't. That's why we couldn't be friends."

"Man, if she isn't a frigging doll," a smiling Dayton tells JJ. "So, what do you do for a living, Miss Gifted Classes?"

I hate how much Dayton loves fucking with people. He can't get enough of sending even the calmest person into a rage.

Bryana wraps her pink hair behind her ears. "I used to work at the bank, but now I'm in sales."

"What's that mean?" Dayton asks, deciding he hasn't irritated anyone to his preferred level yet. "Hookers work in sales, too, but I don't think you're charging for pussy."

JJ laughs, but the humor doesn't reach his eyes. Bryana just looks pissed.

"I sell high-end food."

"She gives out samples at the grocery store," I explain.

A nasty little smile spreads over Dayton's sexy face as his gaze focuses hard on Bryana. I grab his hand to keep him from speaking and making the tension worse.

"So, by high-end food, you meant pizza rolls?" he taunts.

Even though he's the one making digs at her, Bryana glares at me. "What do you do, Harmony?"

"I'm a home health caregiver."

"That's right," Bryana says, snapping her fingers. "I saw you the other day at the grocery store with one of your reta—"

So much for avoiding drama!

My rage switches on in an instant, and I throw a punch before she finishes the hateful word. Bryana tumbles backward as soon as my fist makes contact. Based on her expression, she's nearly as startled as I am.

Next to me, Dayton bursts into laughter. JJ freezes, though, while figuring out the best reaction.

"Ow," I whine, shaking out my hand and shocked by how much my knuckles hurt.

"I'll kiss it better," Dayton says and takes my hand in his.

"I can't believe I hit—"

Bryana dives for me, throwing us both to the dirty ground. My head bounces off the floor. Even stunned, I throw up my arms and prevent her wild hands from clawing my face. Bryana keeps screaming the hateful word and trying to get to my eyes. Suddenly, the weight of her lifts off of me. I look up to find Dayton holding Bryana by the back of her hair.

"Get control of your damn woman," he growls and shoves her toward JJ.

Dayton takes my hand and pulls me up against him. "Catfights are very much appreciated, but you need to learn how to fight better first."

Before I can respond, Bryana appears and slugs me in the eye. My ass hits the floor again, and Dayton grabs her by the throat. I watch them disappear into a crowd of people. New hands pull me to my feet, and I turn to find Mojo Rutgers.

"Hard liquor will fix that right up," he says, checking my swelling eye and then ordering me a shot of tequila.

I don't drink what he puts in front of me. Scanning the crowd, I need Dayton to get me out of Salty Peanuts. I've been in the bar for less than ten minutes, and I've already started a fight I couldn't finish. This place is an even worse influence on me than Dayton.

Appearing from the crowd, my sexy troublemaker struts to the bar. His smirk fades when he spots his dad at my side.

"You smack around JJ's whore?" Mojo asks.

"I don't lower myself to hitting chicks," Dayton replies, maneuvering me so I'm behind him and away from Mojo. "I asked the club sluts to prove their worth by seeing how much hair they could tear out of the bitch's head. The winner gets to spend the night with you, so I'd clear your calendar, Papa."

A smiling Mojo nods at his son's comment before disappearing to wherever the catfight occurs. JJ remains silent throughout the entire incident. I catch him watching Dayton in the same way a cat studies a distracted bird.

My face, head, and ass throb in pain. The bar is too loud, and I'm overheated. Nothing is going the way I wanted, and I need to end this date before making my situation worse.

I grip Dayton's shirt and tug, so he'll look at me. "Take me home, or I'll never go out with you again."

"Threatening me is never smart," he says, rubbing his thumb over my swelling cheek.

"Dayton, please, please, please take me home. I don't want to be here. I've made a fool of myself, and my face hurts."

"How about your pretty noggin?" he asks, reaching around to run his fingers over the back of my head. "Don't want you forgetting my name or the best sexual positions."

"Is this your way of saying you won't take me home, and I'll need to bum a ride from someone else?"

Dayton gives me a nasty little smile. I'm ready for him to make me do more squirming before he gives in.

"Let's ditch this place before JJ's stalker-staring drills a hole in the back of my head."

I peek around Dayton to find his cousin indeed still watching us.

"He's probably pissed about me starting a fight with his girlfriend," I say.

Laughing, Dayton takes my hand and tugs me out of the bar. "Girlfriend," he snorts. "So fucking romantic."

We arrive at his Harley, where he surveys the intersection where Baltimore Street connects with Vine Road. This part of town isn't safe for average people at night. Too many bars liquoring up losers before sending them into the world to act out their drunken frustrations.

A guy like Dayton doesn't need to worry about angry drunks, but he still scans the night looking for trouble. With his hawk-like gaze, he's a predator in search of prey. He might want to hunt, but I only want to go home, cuddle up on my couch with Keanu, and watch "Finding Nemo." Instead, I'm nursing a growing headache on a dangerous street with a guy uninterested in calling it a night.

NINE — DAYTON

I return Harmony to the Lush Gardens Trailer Park. After climbing off the back of my Harley, she pats my shoulder in the way my grandma did when she felt sorry for me.

"Tonight was a disaster," Harmony announces, holding a hand to her eye. "Let's take this clusterfuck as a sign to end things now."

Climbing off the bike, I shake my head. "Nope. Do you think you could ride my girl on your own?"

Harmony frowns at my question, immediately grimacing in pain. "I'm going inside."

"Sounds good."

When I begin to follow her, Harmony presses her hand against my chest.

"You're a bad influence, and I'm too old to be a wild child."

"I'm a bad influence?" I challenge, capturing her hand against my chest. "Don't put this on me. I'm not the hellion who started a fight and then flirted with my dad."

"I did *not* flirt."

"That's not what people were saying."

"What people?"

"The ones living in my head."

Harmony smiles slightly, wanting to find the humor in tonight's clusterfuck. She doesn't give in to her desire, though. "I'd like to put ice on my face and crawl into bed and sleep."

"Should you sleep with a concussion?"

"I don't have a concussion."

"What, so you're a doctor now?"

Harmony rolls her green eyes and walks away. I follow her because there's nowhere I want to be except with my woman.

"Dayton, go home," she says over her shoulder while never slowing down.

"You have peanut shells stuck to your butt."

Harmony stops, wipes the back of her jeans, and then walks again without looking at me. "Tonight was a mess."

"I blame the pink-haired whore."

Even without seeing her face, I know Harmony rolls her eyes. I think she might be grinning, too, but her face is stony when we arrive at her trailer.

"Keanu is still up."

"It's only eight, so that seems about right."

"I can't mess around with you tonight."

"You really like the word 'mess,' don't you?"

"Will you please leave?" she asks, dodging my hands running up her arms.

"No."

Harmony wants to glare at me, but her eye is swelling. She also likely hears her mom coming.

Sally Slater opens the trailer door and scowls at us. "What's this?"

"What's what?" I ask.

"You're back early," she says and then looks closer at Harmony's face. "Did he hit you? Do I need to get my gun?"

Harmony opens her mouth to respond but shuts up once her kid appears next to Sally.

"Mama's home!" he announces and reaches for her.

The next few seconds are a blur. Harmony bolts under Sally's outstretched arm, takes her boy, and hurries into the trailer. Though I try to follow, Mama Bear Slater decides to cock-block.

"Go home," demands the dark-haired beauty.

"Are we throwing down, Sally Slater?"

"You couldn't take me," she growls between clenched teeth.

"I've taken down tougher women than you."

"Name five."

As much as I admire a woman calling my bluff, I refuse to leave.

"Crap, is she bleeding?" I ask, looking over Sally's head to where Harmony stands in the kitchen.

Sally takes the bait and turns away to check on her daughter. I use this moment to gain access to the trailer.

"Oh, must have been the lighting," I say to a frowning Sally.

Harmony sits on the couch, kicks off her shoes, and smiles at Keanu.

"Mama got in a fight," Harmony says when he points at her face. "Fighting is bad."

The boy climbs on the couch next to Harmony and stares at her. She smiles for her kid and tries to make light of her swelling eye. Keanu's little mouth turns down, and he'll wail soon. I can't handle him crying and then Harmony crying. Tears aren't my deal, so I shove a handful of ice from the freezer into a clean kitchen towel.

"Here, kid," I say, sitting next to Harmony and handing the wrapped ice to Keanu. "Put it on her eye and make your mom feel better."

The nearly-crying boy looks at the towel for only a second before grabbing it. He surprises me by smiling.

"Like this?" he asks Harmony and presses the ice on her face. "Better?"

"Yes, baby. You're a great helper."

Keanu watches her expression to make sure she isn't lying. Though I watch her, too, I'm waiting for a sign I'm not in the doghouse.

"Who did you fight with?" Sally asks from the doorway.

"A girl from school."

"And you just stood there and let it happen?" Sally asks me.

Stretching my legs, I look around the trailer and notice the drapes, pillows, and couch cover. "It's purple in here."

"I like purple."

"Do you like purple?" I ask Keanu, who glances between his mom, his grandma, and me.

Though the kid nods, Harmony frowns at me. "Why are you still here?"

"You said we could hang out tonight. Did you lie?"

Harmony looks to her mother for help, and Sally instantly glares at me. Her angry expression would have more power if women didn't always give me dirty looks.

"How's your head?" I ask, reaching over to run my fingers down her soft hair.

"I'm absolutely fine. I plan to spend the rest of my evening watching a movie with Keanu and Mom."

"I like movies," I say, refusing to take the hint.

Ignoring me, Harmony turns on "Finding Nemo" and cuddles with her kid. Sally watches us for nearly an hour. I ignore both the pissed mom glaring at me and the fish movie. My only interest is Harmony, who I stare at unflinchingly.

Occasionally, she glances at me and frowns at how I'm gawking. I only smile because she has no idea how many nights I've spent wishing I could look at her like I am now.

Keanu conks out around the time the father and son fish have their reunion. Watching the little man drool on his mom's lap, I'm more than a little jealous. I'd love to slobber all over Harmony. In fact, I start thinking about how close her bedroom is to where we're currently sitting.

Once Sally carries the kid to bed, I scoot over and wrap an arm around Harmony. "We're alone."

"In this particular room, but my son is so very close by."

"I don't get why you're mad at me. I helped you out when you got in over your head with that dumb bitch. I'm the hero here."

"I'm not mad at you," she says, turning to look at me. "I just can't pretend that you and I make sense as a couple."

"Attraction is primal. Nothing about it needs to make sense."

Using her good eye, Harmony studies my face. Her other eye hides under the towel, even though the ice long ago melted.

"I like you, Dayton, and I have for a long time. But I'm a mother, and Keanu is everything to me. I also have my job and family to take care of. That doesn't leave time for anyone else."

"I'm not anyone else."

"I can't date you."

"Fine, then marry me. That way, I'll have access to you whenever I want."

Harmony instantly stands up. "You're impossible. Get out of my trailer."

Standing up, I take the cloth out of her hand and throw it into the kitchen sink. I smile at my perfect shot and then at Harmony's perfect face.

"What's this really about?" I ask, forcing her hand back into mine.

"I'm not a wild woman. I don't drink and party and go crazy over men."

"Good. Men are awful. You should only go crazy for me."

"I can't fit in your life, and I know you don't fit in mine."

"Then change your life, and I'll change mine."

Harmony gets a stubborn frown on her face. "You need to leave."

"You don't think I can be good with your kid, but I was fine with him tonight."

"You spoke to him once."

Cupping her jaw, I smile. "Yeah, I kept him from bawling like a baby when he got spooked about your eye. That was some good parenting there."

. Harmony fights a smile, and I watch her struggle to remain serious. "Keanu is a baby. He saw his mom with a messed-up face. That fight never would have happened if she hadn't gone out with a wild man she should have kept at a distance from until her kid was in high school. Or maybe college."

"Wild man, huh?" I ask, caressing her plump lips.

"Yes." Harmony steps out of my reach and walks to the trailer door. "Thank you for taking me out tonight. I'm sorry things didn't work out. Maybe we can have fun again some night, but dating makes no sense."

"What did I tell you about attraction and thinking?"

Harmony presses on my chest and shoves me out of the door. I let her pretend she's strong enough to make me do something I don't want. Well, just until she tries to shut the door on me.

"If you kiss me goodnight, I'll leave. If you don't, I'll stay out here and howl at the moon. What's it going to be, Miss Sensible?"

Harmony exhales loudly in the same way my mom used to when I got in trouble at school. Just like back then, the pissed woman relents under the power of my charming smile.

Leaning forward, she plants a kiss on my lips. *A quick kiss. A pity kiss.* Harmony has it all planned in her pretty head.

Except I have plans, too. My hands are ready to keep her from fleeing. Holding Harmony in place, I deepen the kiss and remind her tongue what mine offers.

Harmony doesn't struggle. She kisses me back while her hands slide across my shirt. I feel her teasing my chest hairs through the fabric. Before I can enjoy her seduction, she pulls at them hard enough for me to let her go.

"Why are you always so quick to violence?" I ask, licking my lips.

"You bring out the worst in me."

Smiling, I stretch my arms in the air. "I'll work on that before our next date."

"There will be no more dates."

Shuffling backward, I shake out my arms before adjusting my hard dick in my jeans. "Can't deny the attraction. Don't even try."

Harmony opens her mouth to complain about how I'm not listening. Or maybe she wants to tell me another thing I don't want to hear. Whatever she intends, I wave at her and head to the parking lot.

Nothing she says will change the fact that she's mine. I know it. Sooner or later, she'll know, too. I just need to find a way to make her stop thinking so much. Oh, and keep her away from bitches in bars. As problems go, I've faced worse.

TEN — HARMONY

Walking into a new group home is always nerve-wracking. The average client doesn't care if it's my first day. They expect me to stick to their routine, so I need to hit the ground running as soon as I enter the house.

With this group home, I'm not walking in blind. I've picked up shifts here on occasion. I know enough about the three girls to feel semi-comfortable. That doesn't mean they're relaxed with me.

All three young women have autism, but they're as different as I am from my sisters. Ava wants to eat constantly and will ask for cookies every five minutes. Jaylee will spin for hours if no one distracts her. She's also a bit of a klepto, so I need to keep an eye on her entering the other girls' rooms. Then, there's Millie.

The tall, thin, twenty-year-old looks at me warily when I first enter her room. If she remembers me from previous visits, she doesn't show it. Millie scratches my arms when I help her in the shower. She smacks me upside the head when I get her dressed. Mostly, she squawks and stomps her feet, wanting me to leave her alone.

I don't get upset. She's territorial about her room, not unlike most people about their private space. Millie just isn't verbal enough to explain why I should fuck off. Instead, she scares people away with her yelling and aggression.

But like her housemates, she's quite charming once she warms up to me. By Friday of my first full week, I've gotten Millie to smile. She also gives me a hug before I leave for the weekend. Knowing I've built a rapport with someone who rarely trusts people makes me feel like a superstar.

Each night that week, Keanu notices the scratches on my arms and neck. His immediate solution to my ouchies is to put ice on them like Dayton showed him with my eye.

"I'm helping," he says, holding the cloth against my arm.

"You're the best helper."

Though Keanu smiles, he doesn't like the scratches and keeps expecting them to go away once he puts the cloth on them.

"I still have my eye ouchie," I say, and he puts the cloth on it.

"Wait, do you have an ouchie on your knee?" I say, pointing to a scrape.

Keanu looks at his knee and shows his LEGO toy, Carl. "I fell down."

"Well, let's put a cloth on it."

"Band-Aid, too," he says, and I already know he thinks that'll fix my scratches.

Soon, I have a Band-Aid just under my eye, plus ones covering my scratched arms and neck. Keanu wears a few Band-Aids, even on spots without injuries. Of course, Carl needs a Band-Aid, too.

In the quiet moments with my baby, I don't think about Dayton. When I'm busy at work, I don't think of him, either. Not when I grocery shop or spend time with my mom and her friends.

Dayton remains absent from my thoughts until I climb into bed every night. Then, I swear I smell him, even though I've washed my sheets. Resting in the dark, I sometimes hear his voice. When I close my eyes, I feel his hot breath on my skin. There are even moments when I sense the bed shift as if his large, long body is moving on it.

Opening my eyes, I'm always alone, and I feel it down to my bones. I've never been a lonely person, but I can't shake the urge to have Dayton in my bed. Worse still, I wonder if he's with another woman but would rather be with me.

However, I refuse to call him. I know how our story ends with me falling hard and Dayton walking away.

ELEVEN — DAYTON

The way to a mother's heart is through her kid. If Harmony plans to use her boy as a cock-blocker, I'll need to get him on my team.

Harmony once said Keanu likes animals and the zoo. She won't let me come along on their outings because she figures I'm a bad influence. That's her bullshit way to keep me at a distance.

I knock on Charlie and Billy's door around noon. Lush Gardens is quiet except for an argument a lane or two over from this one. I hear the woman screaming at her husband over him being a deadbeat. He calls her a whore who never earned a cent in her entire life. I laugh at the stupidity of them arguing over who's the bigger loser.

"Camden?" Charlie says, appearing on the other side of the screen door. "Is something wrong with Daisy?"

The woman is a decade older than her BFF, Sally Slater, and shows it with her gray hair and wrinkled face. Keanu's babysitter might look like the average grandma, but she parties as hard as her friends. I also heard she's quick to pull a gun, so I guess it's a good thing she thinks I'm my brother.

"I'm Dayton, but I won't take that personal."

"Oh, what do you want?"

"I'm taking Keanu to the zoo."

"Says who?" she asks, placing a hand on her hip like my grandma used to when I pissed her off.

"Says the guy with the gun."

"Well, boy, everyone has a gun these days. You wanna see mine?"

"Sure, but I don't think you're going to shoot me. I can't promise I won't do the same."

"You're not going to shoot me, Dayton Rutgers."

"No, maybe not, but I might wing that stupid dog of yours," I say, gesturing to the yappy furry ball staring at me.

"Bullshit."

"Probably. Now, get the kid, and I'll take him to the zoo."

"No."

"Why not?"

"He doesn't know you."

"Whose fault is that? I'm trying to get to know him right now, but you're standing in my way."

"What are you trying to do here?" she asks, walking outside and shutting the screen door so the dog won't follow.

"I told you."

"Harmony won't think you're boyfriend material if you kidnap her boy."

"I'm not kidnapping no one. If I was, then telling you about it ahead of time would be an amateur move."

"Kids are loud and messy. You should find a woman without one."

"I already found those women, and they were shit. Every single one of them. Now, don't go telling me how you know someone who isn't shit. I already found that someone you're talking about, and she was, in fact, shit."

"I'll tell you what," she says, giving my chest a poke. "If you want to take him to the zoo, then you need to take me, too. Otherwise, I can't let you take him without a fight, and I've been hoping to use my new shotgun."

I look her up and down. "All right, but only because I like dogs, and I don't shoot old ladies."

"You're a sugar cookie, aren't you, child?"

"That's what I hear. So, is the kid ready to go?"

Charlie stifles laughter. "You really don't know children if you think he can pop out of the door that fast."

I don't believe it'll be such a hassle. After all, Keanu comes to the door once Charlie calls his name. He's a cute little guy, even if I don't like how his existence always reminds me of how Harmony fucked some asshole.

"Do you want to go to the zoo?" Charlie asks.

His dark eyes light up, and he jumps around. Once Charlie tells him to find his shoes, Keanu bolts into the trailer. I figure we'll be on the road in five minutes tops.

Twenty minutes later, we're finally walking to the parking lot.

"I brought a club SUV since I knew he had to sit in one of these things," I say, jiggling the kiddie chair in my hand.

"You knew that, huh? You're a regular Michael Landon, aren't you?"

"I don't know who that is."

"Of course not. Kids today grew up watching crap."

Ignoring her, I glance back at Keanu under his army green bucket hat. We arrive at the SUV, where I decide to make chit chat with the kid that should be mine.

"Do you like the zoo?" I ask. When he only nods, I turn to Charlie. "Does he talk?"

"You know he does," she mutters, taking the kiddie chair from me and strapping it into the back seat. "He isn't an attention whore seeking out conversation with strangers. Keanu just wants to see the animals."

Climbing into the seat, Keanu waits to be strapped in. Charlie walks around me and gets into the passenger seat, but I don't shut the door.

I study the boy and wonder what he's thinking. Does he care one way or another about the stranger taking him to the zoo? I remember how my cousin, Bonn, used to want a dad in his life. He'd watch fathers with their kids and then get that look in his eyes like a puppy dying for a treat.

Does Keanu ever get that look, too? I don't know anything about kids or how they think at different ages. Could be this one doesn't know about dads yet.

I finally shut the door and walk to the driver's spot. Soon, we're on the highway toward Nashville. Charlie controls the radio channels and ignores me for the ride.

I'm happy for the silence, but I can't help thinking Charlie must have called or messaged Harmony. Will my woman show up at the zoo and admire my fatherly ability? Nope, she'll freak out, but I like it when she gets mad. *Rage is a sexy look on her.*

TWELVE — HARMONY

Millie doesn't allow people close to her, and many staff members have quit after she gave them a hard time. Once she bonds with someone, though, she becomes incredibly attached and loving. With her viewing me as a friend rather than an intruder in her personal space, I'm one of her favorite people.

Leaving work early isn't an option. Yet, I'm about ready to come out of my skin once I read Charlie's texts.

First, she mentions Dayton's visit. Then, she says they're on their way to the zoo. When I call her, she promises I don't need to worry. She and Keanu will enjoy the zoo and even score a free meal out of it. *Isn't that fun?*

My texts to Dayton go unanswered. He once explained how he never answers his phone because doing so encourages people to call him.

"I've got a system, see?" he said, giving me a wink.

I'd thought he was so freaking funny back then. Now, I want to slug him. Well, maybe not since my hand remains tender from punching Bryana. Okay, so I'm not a fighter, but I plan to make that boy pay a serious price for pulling this stunt. *No one messes with my kid.*

The last hour at work is the longest of my life. I stand near Millie's door, peeking in regularly to ensure she hasn't started picking at the healing scratches on her arms. Though I want to clean, the house is pristine. I consider cooking, but the girls already had their snacks. With nothing to keep me busy, I check my phone constantly.

Charlie sends me photos of Keanu pointing at a giraffe and squatting down to see through the bars at the elephants. I get one of Dayton pushing the stroller. There's a picture of them eating a giant ice cream cookie. Followed by a shot of Keanu covered in the giant ice cream cookie. At three years old, he's completely incapable of eating so much food.

In all the pictures, my son looks happy. He isn't scared of Dayton. Keanu's just having fun with Charlie and some guy.

As I leave work and head to the zoo, I receive a picture from Charlie with Keanu and Dayton's faces painted like tigers. *Okay, so they look adorable.* I'm also admittedly impressed Dayton allowed someone to paint all over his manly face when club guys aren't known to be silly.

Still, I refuse to forgive the asshole's behavior. Even if he looks cuter as hell with whiskers. And despite my son is grinning from ear to ear in the pictures. *Nope, I'm mad.* I'm staying mad, too. Dayton has no idea what kind of mama bear instincts he's riled up.

The drive to the zoo takes forever yet goes by in a flash. The entire time, I imagine confronting Dayton. What I'll say to him and how I'll say it all while wearing a smile, so Keanu won't know I'm pissed. I have a whole damn speech planned!

I know exactly where they are, too, after Charlie sends me a photo of Keanu sitting in his stroller and staring at an aquarium. Next to him, Dayton rests on the ground like he owns the freaking place. *Typical Rutgers crap.*

I use my zoo membership pass to hurry through the line. Dodging strollers and toddlers, I nearly run the rest of the way to where my son and not-boyfriend watch tropical fish.

Then, I just stop. The sight of them kills my anger and leaves me confused. For the first time, I ask myself why Dayton would pull this stunt in the first place. *What does he want besides to drive me crazy?*

Charlie appears at my side. "Give me your keys."

"Why?"

"I'll head home, and you can catch a ride back with those two."

"Are you sure?"

Charlie glances at them and nods. "Dayton told Keanu that once you got here, they could have hot dogs for dinner. He's been feeding him all kinds of crap. That man would kill anyone's diet."

"Staying here for hot dogs will only encourage Dayton."

Charlie tries not to laugh in my face. "I don't suspect he needs much encouragement from you. I think the voices in his fat head do that enough already."

Frowning at where Keanu and Dayton still stare at the fish tank, I shake my head. "I screwed up by letting him in my life. Now I don't know how to get him out."

"Dayton's not so bad."

"He showed up at your trailer and wanted to take Keanu to the zoo without even asking me. That's bad, Charlie."

"Yeah, and he made threats and talked tough, but I figured something out about him today."

"What's that?"

"A good half of what comes out of that boy's mouth is utter bullshit. You can't take him literally. I'm not saying you and him are a match made in heaven, but you shouldn't write him off completely. After all, his brother seems like a good husband to Daisy."

"Ugh, don't talk about husbands. I haven't gone on a single successful date with Dayton. He hasn't even reached boyfriend status yet."

"Yet?"

Rolling my eyes, I hand her my keys. "Thanks for dealing with this today."

"It wasn't all bad. He bought me ice cream and a super-sized soda. Coming here was a lot more fun than sitting at the trailer park all day."

Smiling at Charlie's expression, I consider asking her to stay and act as a buffer between Dayton and me. Rather than make a chicken move, I tell her goodbye.

After she leaves, I watch Keanu and Dayton, who are oblivious to me. For a few minutes, I nearly forget how we ended up here. I'm too busy taking in the sight of my sweet boy chilling next to my long-time sexy crush. Despite my common sense, I can't control my smile. That's when I know I'm in trouble.

THIRTEEN — DAYTON

While I never much cared for the zoo as a kid, I can't complain about my day with Keanu. He doesn't bitch and whine. No crying, either. My one complaint is he doesn't say anything. *How am I supposed to show off my daddy abilities with a mute kid?*

When we reach the Tropical Rivers attraction, I ask, "So what are you into?"

"I don't know," he says, giving me a double shoulder shrug.

"What do you like?"

Keanu points at the tank in front of us. "Fish."

"That it?"

"LEGOs," he says, showing me the little toy man he's held the entire day.

"You like building stuff, huh?"

Keanu only nods while staring at the fish like a stalker on the hunt. I study his face, looking for Harmony in his features. Despite knowing I take after my mom, I see only Mojo when I look in the mirror.

"Building is cool. I built a house one summer to help our club brother after a storm knocked his place down. Cool shit, but I wouldn't do it for a job, you know?"

Keanu doesn't react to my words. He's in awe of the fish swimming back and forth in the giant tank. I plop on my ass and sit next to him on the ground. The people around us mutter about me acting like a rude fucker. I only smile because annoying people is my crack.

"You know who I think is cool?" I ask, and he does his double shoulder shrug again. "Your mom. She's my favorite person."

Keanu instantly smiles. Seeing Harmony in his expression, I share his grin.

"She's a cool chick. I want to keep hanging out with her. You cool with that?"

44

Though Keanu nods, I don't think he's listening. I'm used to people ignoring me, so I don't take it personally. Especially not with a three-year-old. I remember when Hudson was little, and everyone thought he was deaf because he didn't react to them. My brother was barely out of the womb when he learned to con people.

We watch the fish for twenty minutes before I hear a voice I know from my dreams. Glancing back at Charlie sitting on a bench, I see a wisp of blonde hair. Knowing Harmony will soon read me the riot act, I look back at the fish and enjoy the quiet before the storm.

Harmony doesn't rush over to us. When she does show up, she dips her head around the stroller and whispers into Keanu's ear. The boy's dark eyes light up as he touches her worried face.

"Are you okay?" she asks.

"I don't see the blue fish," he says. "Where did it go?"

"I don't know, baby."

Harmony kneels next to the stroller and gives me a pissed look. "What are you doing?"

"I wanted to see if I could get along with your kid without you around to entertain me."

"What gives you that right?"

"I'm a spoiled man, Harmony. No one hands me anything. I expect it, and I take it. The good news is Keanu and I got along fine. We're eating hot dogs pretty soon."

Keanu studies his mom before climbing out of the stroller. He reaches for her, and Harmony instantly picks him up. The kid rests his head on her shoulder and smiles like he's her biggest fan.

"Did you look at the piranha?" Harmony whispers.

Keanu whispers something back. And just like that, I'm on the outside looking in.

Watching Harmony cuddle with her son makes my dick hard for some reason. I think it's because she's extra sexy when she smiles, and her family never fails to make her happy.

I need to make her smile like that, too. Not just in bed, either. I can fuck a grin on her face day and night. Yet, that

45

won't keep her from dismissing me as a mistake she doesn't want to make again.

FOURTEEN — HARMONY

I ignore Dayton while Keanu shows me his favorite fish. We see if we can name all of the piranhas for next time. I walk with my baby while Dayton pushes along the empty stroller. More than once, I consider looking back at him. Except I'm not in the mood to see him pout. Dayton's sad face brings out my mama bear instincts, inspiring me to give him anything to make him smile again.

"I'm sticky," Keanu says, showing me his shirt.

"That's why we have bath time."

He smiles at me and then looks back at Dayton. "We have paint on our face."

I finally relent and look at Dayton with his tiger-painted face. The orange color emphasizes his dark brown eyes, and the red brings out his miserable frown.

"You both look adorable," I say, cupping Keanu's face and then Dayton's.

I get a smile out of them both. Dayton's makes me immediately regret my kind gesture. *The pompous ass is back on the prowl.*

"Your kid couldn't handle a whole cookie."

"He's three," I say, narrowing my eyes and flashing him my meanest look.

Dayton leans closer and whispers, "Stop flirting in front of the boy."

Rolling my eyes, I turn away and take Keanu's hand. We spend another twenty minutes looking at the fish and naming the pretty ones. Though Dayton offers a few options, I ignore his suggestions. After all, we're naming fish, not strippers.

"Who's hungry?" Dayton announces when we finish the Tropical Rivers attraction.

Keanu jumps. "Me!"

I smile at how excitable my baby gets about the smallest things. He's a ray of sunshine walking around in a little boy's body. Lifting my gaze to Dayton watching me, my smile falters. While Keanu offers me simple joys, this man comes with a long list of complications.

"I could eat," I tell him.

"Well, then, little man, why don't you jump in your stroller? Then, we'll round up hot dogs."

My baby darts into the stroller. Dayton wraps an arm around my shoulders and then pushes Keanu to the food court.

"Ain't this cozy," he whispers in my ear as we maneuver around people.

"Today, you crossed a line. I'll play nice for Keanu's sake. However, after we eat, you'll take us home and then go the fuck away."

"So young and naïve."

"You suck."

"Ah, you do remember our night together," he says, smiling wider. "I'll do that tonight until you howl at the moon."

"What's with you and howling at the moon?"

"I dig werewolf movies."

"I'm sorry I asked. Let's just eat and go our separate ways."

"Again, with your youthful naïveté. What's it like to see the world through rose-colored glasses? It's fun, isn't it?"

"What does that mean?"

"You can't get away from me," he whispers menacingly. "I'll never give up until I claim you as mine. You can run, and you can hide, but I'll find you, and I'll make you submit. If you see any other ending to this, you're living in a fantasy land with unicorns and fairy farts."

We arrive at the food court and find an empty table. I get Keanu in a seat and then shove myself up against Dayton.

"I'm not scared of you, buddy. Quit threatening me. Stop pulling stupid stunts. And for fuck's sake, stop pretending I'm a girlish teenager who's never met a big strong man like you. I'm a mom, and I've fucked more guys than you have brain cells. Now go get us hot dogs."

"Fries, too?"

"Sure."

Dayton glares at me. "What kind of crap does the kid drink?"

"Juice."

"I'll be back."

"Fine."

I hold my frown until Dayton is in line. Sitting next to Keanu, I run my fingers over his.

"Did you have fun today?"

"Yeah."

"Was Dayton nice to you?"

"He's funny."

"Funny how?"

"He said the elephant smelled."

"Well, they do smell."

"He said it funny."

I glance at Dayton, who stares at the menu as if it's printed in a different language.

Focusing back on Keanu, I sigh. "Whose idea was it to get your face painted?"

"Charlie wanted it."

"Did Dayton whine like a baby?"

"No. He was brave."

I smile at how serious Keanu says the words. "Did you like your big cookie?"

"It melted."

"Yeah, they melt fast."

"I made a mess," he says, showing off his sticky shirt again.

"Did Dayton get mad at you for not eating it fast enough?"

While Keanu shakes his head, he's focused on the big scary biker man approaching with a tray of food.

"Hot dogs," Keanu says, full of awe.

"I got two juices. One is for the ride home," Dayton says, handing them to Keanu.

"Thanks," I tell him, and he catches my softer tone.

"Someone isn't so naïve anymore."

49

Rolling my eyes, I want to be angry, but Keanu is too happy for his good mood not to rub off on me.

We eat our food while talking about animals. While I'm relieved to keep the conversation light, I know what's waiting for me once we return to Lush Gardens.

The minute I get Keanu into the trailer, I turn to Dayton and hold him back from entering.

"We will try going on a date one more time. This Friday, you can pick me up. If it sucks, we are done. Stalk me all you want afterward, but I won't bend."

"You'll bend," he says without hesitation.

"I guess we'll find out, won't we?"

"Naw," he says, cupping the back of my head and pulling me closer. "I'm going to knock you off your feet on Friday. No way will you want to get back up."

Dayton kisses me hard, deep, and ends it with a nip at my bottom lip. Despite my shivering body wanting to keep him locked in my bedroom forever, I shrug with indifference.

"See you Friday."

Grinning like a predator, Dayton steps away from me. "Tell the little man I said, 'later gator.'"

Even giving him a smile, I'm dreading Friday. Dayton knows how to get me worked up, and I'm aching to let loose. As much as he seems like the perfect guy to go wild with, I'm fully aware of the baggage Dayton drags behind him.

FIFTEEN — DAYTON

My mother is the youngest Hallstead sister in a town where the name means something. Unlike her childless spinster sisters—who just happen to be the town's mayor and sheriff—Clara found love twice and produced three sons. I like to believe I'm the best of the bunch, but I often sense I'm the only one with that opinion.

Mom married a wild man the first time around, but Mojo wasn't the settling down type. Despite his inability to keep his dick in his pants, I don't think he wanted out of the marriage. He often says Mom was a good wife, and marriage suited him.

Mojo's mistake was thinking his young bride would put up with his crap. Apparently, her undying love didn't kill her common sense, so she ditched him.

Now, she's married to a retired military man who doesn't say much and always keeps his dick in the marital bed. I'd say she traded up with Erik. He's even a good father to my younger brother, Hudson, who's just as quiet and odd.

Despite being a grown man, I can drop by Mom's house whenever I want and eat her food, sleep on her couch, and ask her to do my laundry. She pretends like she loves the entire thing, and I act like I believe her lies.

Walking into the big house on the hill—as the locals call it—I hope Mom's baked a pie or cake. I stayed up too late drinking the night before, and the sugar might be the only thing to keep me awake.

"It's still in the oven," Mom says, looking up from her book. "You'll need to be patient. Erik and Hud finished off the one from last night."

"Ungrateful pigs," I mutter, making a beeline to the couch. "Are they around?"

"They're out back training. Want to join them?"

I catch Mom smirking. She knows I'm hungover and grumpy. No way do I want to run around an obstacle course and play soldier.

"Do you ever have regrets?" I ask while using one of her fancy pillows to cover my face from the sun.

"Sure. I regret not putting the pie in earlier, so you'd have something to eat when you arrived."

I smile under the pillow. "I also regret that."

"Are you staying for dinner?"

"I don't know. I'm waiting for a call to see what my plans are for the night."

"Dayton, didn't your daddy ever teach you not to make a woman feel like she's your second choice?"

"He didn't teach me much of anything. Well, besides how to ride a bike and shave."

"You crash that thing all the time and rarely shave. I'd say Adam did a sloppy job."

Grinning under the pillow, I get around to asking the question Mojo's been pushing for weeks. "Are you still pissed about De Campo's?"

"Among other things," Mom says, setting aside her book. "What are your first choice plans?"

"I'm sure you've already heard I'm chasing Harmony Slater."

"I'd say you were copying your brother by hooking up with one of Sally's girls. However, I know you've been sniffing around Harmony for years."

"She does smell good."

"Do you think she'll let you catch her?"

"I don't know. Maybe, but I'm not sure she sees me correctly."

"You shouldn't want a woman who won't see the real you. I imagined things in your father that weren't there. We know how that worked out."

"Yeah, you birthed two handsome sons."

"You are handsome boys," Mom says, giving me a proud smile.

"Do you regret marrying him?"

52

"No, I regret trusting him. That and thinking a woman like me won't get cheated on by a man like him. I was too full of myself back in the day. So, spill, Dayton. What are you regretting?"

I don't answer right away because I hate admitting I fucked up. Like Mom, I'm a big fan of myself. My ego demands I never own up to my failings.

"Years ago, I was at a party with Harmony, and she gave me the green light. All I had to do was promise I wouldn't treat her like shit afterward. I don't know why, but I couldn't say the words. I guess I didn't want to lie, and I didn't know what I'd do after we banged."

"Banged," Mom sighs. "You *are* your father's son."

"I know, so do you want to hear the fucked-up part?"

"Sure."

"I bailed on her, and she ended up meeting a dorky foreign guy. Somehow, he got the green light, and they made her kid. That could have been my kid. Instead, he's the son of a dead guy who isn't even around to help out."

"I think you'd be a good father."

Her words surprise me. Pulling back the pillow from my eyes, I frown. "Really?"

"You were always good with Hudson when he was little. Camden made sure Hud followed the rules, but you made sure he was happy."

"It's true I'm better than Cam."

Mom smiles. "You're different."

"I fucked up that night with Harmony. I wanted her, but I wasn't sure I'd only want her. I think that's what she wanted from me. A kind of commitment where I could be a boyfriend she could depend on. I'd never done the boyfriend routine, and I figured I shouldn't practice on the girl I actually wanted. So, I walked away. Who'd have thought some computer geek would swoop in?"

"I still don't understand what she saw in him."

"He was into supernatural crap like her. Harmony probably thought he was the kind of guy she should want, not an asshole like me."

"You *can* be an asshole at times."

Nodding, I add, "I look at her kid and think about how he could have been mine if I weren't a fucking idiot."

"You weren't ready then. If you were, he would be yours. Harmony would be, too."

"I was a grown man too scared to make a promise to a chick I'd been chasing since she was jailbait."

"You really should learn to edit yourself, Dayton," Mom says, walking to the kitchen. "You turn beautiful sentiments into tawdriness."

"I don't believe in thinking before I speak."

"That's not true, and we both know it."

Sitting up, I join her in the kitchen. "No, I guess it's not. I lie with a lot of people. I guess I could do that with women. Do you want me to lie to you?"

"Yes."

After we share a smile, I stand over Mom while she takes the pie from the oven. She pushes me away when I get too close.

"It's hot."

"What kind did you make?"

"Your favorite. I must have known you were coming over."

Hugging her against me, I sigh. "Why can't life be as fucking simple as what pie my mommy makes?"

"Because you're a big strong man who needs to worry about big strong man things."

Refusing to let go of my mom, I wish I were a kid again, and she could make my problems go away. My big mouth got me into trouble plenty of times growing up, and Mom always smoothed things over.

Too bad I can't send her to Harmony to fix things. Or send her back in time to tell the old Dayton to promise Harmony whatever necessary to make her mine that night.

SIXTEEN — HARMONY

Nearly a decade ago, Ruby and Bonn broke up after he cheated one night while she was pregnant. Now, they've finally patched things up and plan to get married. I'm thrilled, much like when Daisy got hitched with Camden.

However, I miss having my sisters at the trailer park. We used to walk back and forth so much the entire lane felt like our private home.

Now, they live in the same condo building as Dayton. As I arrive with Keanu, I think of the sexy bad man down the hall. He's probably asleep since it's before noon.

Ruby answers the door, sees my worried face, and reacts with concern. Then, she remembers Keanu is watching her and throws on a smile.

Keanu holds my hand until we're in the condo. "Can I play?" he asks Ruby.

Elle appears from her room and waves Keanu over. My boy takes off running.

"He misses her so much," I tell Ruby while smiling at Daisy nearby.

Despite my casual tone, I know my sisters are watching me. On the phone, I mentioned I got into an argument at the bar. Yet, I skipped the violence part of the story.

"What the heck?" Daisy asks, cupping my face.

"I told you what happened with Bryana."

"You didn't say she hit you."

"I hit her first."

"What?" Ruby balks. "You're non-violent. A wuss. A hippy without a mean bone in your body."

"You're just making crap up."

"Well, you've never gotten in a fight before."

Daisy nods. "Even when girls were vicious toward you in school, you didn't pound them. Not even when I encouraged you to."

"Bryana was going to say the R-word, and you know how that makes me mad."

"I've never seen you punch someone for saying it, though."

"Okay, so Dayton is a bad influence."

Daisy gives me a disappointed scowl. "Did he egg you on? If so, how come you listened to him and not to me?"

"Dayton didn't do anything. Instead, his wild way of thinking infected me, and I lost my mind."

"Did he offer you sex if you punched her? I can't do that," Daisy says, not letting up on how she wanted me to fight girls in the past.

"I don't know how to explain it," I mutter, sitting at the kitchen table. "I felt different when I was on the back of his Harley. We got there, and I saw her, and she said that, and I let go of the part of me that thinks about consequences. I punched her, and then she jumped me. That's when I realized that for a wild child, I fight like poop."

"You mean she won?" Daisy cries.

"Dayton dragged her off me. I'm still shocked that I hit someone."

"It hurt your hand, didn't it?" Ruby asks.

"Heck yeah, it does. My knuckles are bruised from the one hit. I don't know how Dayton goes around punching people all the time."

"Practice," Ruby says, running her fingers over my knuckles.

"So, are you and Dayton a thing now?" Daisy asks.

"No, I bailed on our Friday date. He threatened to take Keanu somewhere else fun. I threatened to harm his ball sack. Then, he said he would need to harass me from now on."

Ruby nods. "Sounds like him. Though I'm still freaked out by the Keanu zoo thing."

"He wanted to prove he could be good with my kid."

"Was he good with him?"

Smiling, I nod. "You saw the painted face pictures. I don't know if that means he'd be a good father figure, but he clearly knows how to act like a little kid."

56

"Okay, we all know Dayton is an impulsive jerk sometimes," Daisy says. "But what matters is if you're still interested in him. So, are you?"

"I'll always be interested in him. The guy's my sexy ideal. However, that doesn't change how he's Dayton Rutgers, and I'm a mom. We're not a match made in long-term relationship heaven."

"Why worry about whether you make sense?" Daisy pushes, probably thinking about future double dates.

"You did when you were dating Camden."

"Yeah, and look at how that turned out."

"Camden's the boring twin," Ruby says, smiling in anticipation of Daisy's irritation. "Dayton is a drunk and a slut. He doesn't possess the family man gene. The man took a child he doesn't know to the zoo without your permission. He has some growing up to do."

"He's like his dad that way," I say, but Daisy shakes her head.

"Dayton is a mama's boy."

"Says who?"

"Says me."

"Well, you are very wise," I tease while moving to the couch in the living room. "Let's talk about something else."

"Nope. I don't think you should have bailed on having dinner with Dayton. You need to go on a real date," Daisy says, standing behind me. Her fingers twist my hair into a messy braid. "No bars or club stuff. Go on a normal date and see what he's like outside of that world."

Ruby sits in a nearby chair. "She isn't totally wrong. It wasn't Dayton who made you throw the punch at the bar. That was you. Learn a little self-control, wild child."

"Hey, I didn't screw him that night or after the zoo. I'd say I have a whole lot of self-control."

"That's true," Daisy says, joining me on the couch. "He looks just like Camden, and we all know my man's unbelievably sexy."

Ruby frowns. "Cool your jets, horndog."

"Sorry, but I cannot lie. I married a hottie."

"So did he," I tell Daisy. "Never forget that."

"I probably will so be sure to remind me a lot. My ego preemptively thanks you."

Smiling, I bump her leg with my foot. "Now, can we talk about something else?"

"Only if you promise to do one legit date with Dayton before blowing him off. I mean, how perfect would it be if you two fell in love and lived down the hall from us?"

Ruby smiles at this thought. "Elle would love having her best friend down the hall."

"Uh, I'll try dinner, but we shouldn't get our hopes up. Dayton isn't a man looking to settle down. Now, let's talk about something fun like Ruby's wedding."

My sister stands up and walks to the kitchen, clearly uninterested in our new topic.

"The wedding part doesn't interest me," she says while I peek in on Keanu and Elle. I find the two playing with LEGOs and talking about cats. Back in the kitchen, Ruby checks on lunch. "I want to put the money and effort into a fun reception. Something the kids can enjoy."

"Are you thinking about having it at La Famiglia?" Daisy asks while stretching out on the couch.

"Have you ever heard of the term 'don't shit where you eat'?"

"So where, then?" I ask. "Wait, is this your way of smoothing us into the idea of having the reception at Chuck E. Cheese?"

I smile when Daisy snickers at the thought. Ruby ignores the question, too busy finishing lunch.

"Where were you thinking?" I ask, joining Ruby in the kitchen.

Removing the ham and cheese quesadillas from the oven, she sets them on the stove and looks them over. "The Boogie Bowl."

"Mom and the girls will love that," I say and then grab her shirt. "Will it be a 1980s-themed reception?"

"Yep," she says, smiling. "The kids love dancing, and the Boogie Bowl has a karaoke machine. It's not too expensive to reserve for a private party. I think it'll be fun for our family."

Hugging Ruby, I whisper in her ear, "Don't shortchange yourself. Not on the wedding or the reception. Don't focus on making everyone else happy. You earned this with Bonn, and you should spoil yourself."

"We're thinking about trying for a baby soon," she whispers back. "I don't want to be extravagant with a ceremony or party right now. I'm thinking about the future." Ruby cups my face and adds, "But thank you for thinking of me. As moms, we sometimes forget to pamper ourselves."

Smiling, I hear the hidden meaning in Ruby's words. The night at Salty Peanuts, I'd been on edge and likely looking for trouble. When Bryana appeared with her bitchy bigotry, I created a situation to prove Dayton, and I don't make sense. Without a lick of planning, I sabotaged us before we even ordered a drink.

While the food cools down, I walk down the hallway to Dayton's door. He doesn't answer my knock despite being home.

Ringing the bell, I know he's likely passed out inside the condo. Sooner or later, he'll shuffle to the door, and I won't leave until that happens.

After a few minutes, Dayton opens the door and stares at me through fatigued eyes. "Harmony Slater, your tits look like absolute perfection in that shirt. Did you wear it for me?"

"Are you alone?" I ask, peering around him into the condo. "Why is it so dark in there?"

"I hate the sun."

"You didn't answer if you were alone."

"Who would be here?"

"A woman."

"Do women besides you even exist?" he asks, leaning against the doorjamb and testing the power of his boxer's elastic.

I stare at how the gray fabric threatens to drop past his strong hips. Dayton glances down at where I'm focused.

"You can yank 'em down if you want."

"No, I'm good."

"If you're not here for sex, what'd you wake me up for?"

"I bailed on your dinner invitation."

"Yeah, I remember that coward move, but I've already forgiven you," he says, running his finger along the curve of my shirt just above my breasts.

"I want to reschedule."

Dayton gives me a sly smile. "Of course, you do."

"Are you really in there alone?"

"Stop asking me that question," he says, losing his grin. "If I were banging a whore, I wouldn't have her stay over."

"What do you mean by 'if'?"

"My dick craves only the nice blonde lady standing in front of it. Maybe she'll give it a kiss before she goes."

Rolling my eyes, I step back. "Sorry, penis, but my sisters and Keanu are waiting for me. I'm only here to make plans for Friday."

"I'll pick you up at six. Don't bail again, or I'll chase you down."

"I'll see you then," I say, backing away while staring at his erection barely hidden by those gray boxers. "If you're good on Friday, your friend might get a kiss after all."

Dayton glances down at his hard-on and nods approvingly. I leave him before we end up doing something horribly inappropriate. In fact, I nearly run to Ruby's door to prevent me from returning to Dayton and his erection.

Friday can't come soon enough.

SEVENTEEN — DAYTON

My uncle likes pussy as much as he hates condoms. There's no other way of explaining why Howler has so many bastard kids in the world. Most of them stay on the DL, likely hoping for an inheritance once he kicks the bucket.

Growing up, I knew Bonn was my cousin. We went to the same schools and became friends, but he wasn't invited to family functions. I do know my mom sent him gifts for his birthdays and Christmases. I'm also fairly certain the Hallstead sisters sent checks on occasion to ensure the boy was fed and clothed.

Otherwise, Howler's bastards stayed away. That is, until a few months back, when Jude Junior arrived in Hickory Creek Township, looking to meet his long-lost dad. To most people's surprise, Howler welcomed this bastard with open arms.

For me, it wasn't such a shock. I'd noticed my uncle's mind slipping a year before JJ ever showed up. The middle-aged fucker got shaky during fights. He drank too much, laughed too loud, and his taste in women got so young it bordered on illegal. I called a midlife crisis on Howler long before he became silly proud over JJ.

I'm probably the only other person in Hickory Creek who's cool with my newest cousin. Camden views JJ as an interloper, trying to take what's rightfully his. The Hallstead women blame him for the fire that destroyed a restaurant they wanted saved. Bonn sees his half-brother enjoying the kind of attention from Howler that the old man never gave him.

JJ's managed to irritate pretty much everyone in the club and even the old ladies. Pissing off the wives is a loser move, but JJ got it done. *The man has a talent.*

JJ doesn't look like much. He's wiry, and his shoulder-length hair is thin. Despite his size, he's a mean fucker who's taken down plenty of bigger guys. Mostly because he's sneaky and willing to shiv someone when they're not looking.

"Heard you hooked up with that blonde Slater girl," he says, joining me at the back booth at our club hangout, Salty Peanuts. "Camden's sister-in-law."

"Heard that, did you? I guess you're part of the gossip bunch in Hickory Creek now."

"People talk," he says, ordering a beer.

"Sure, but I hook up with a lot of women. Blondes, redheads, brunettes. Once I porked a chubby girl with purple hair. She was a wild one."

"Those Slater girls sure know how to marry up."

Normally, I shrugged off JJ's bullshit, even when it touched on Camden and Daisy. Except he's bitching about Harmony now. "Why you got a bug up your ass about pretty trailer park girls doing well in life?"

"No. None of that shit. I just believe in calling out a gold digger when I see one."

"I don't doubt the Slater girls have been called worse, but I dig Harmony," I say without sounding too hung up about her and no doubt fooling this stupid shit. "She and I have been friends with some benefits for years. So, watch the way you call her out around me. I don't want to take anything personal. That's not my style. Yet, she's a great lay, so who knows what could happen if you cross a line?"

"Never thought I'd see you get stupid over a woman."

"Don't call me names unless you're willing to bring me a tissue for my tears, asshole."

Though JJ smiles, his grins always feel like a put-on. I don't need to be psychic to know the man is boiling over with rage at the world. When it spills over, I wonder who will get the privilege of ending him. If he keeps talking shit about Harmony, I'll be at the front of the line to make him dead.

"Mojo says we got to put you through the paces and get you patched in," I tell JJ since he's eyeing me like a grifter studying his newest mark.

"I'm ready to be a brother to you."

I fight the urge to roll my eyes. This asshole doesn't know two shits about loyalty and family. I bet he'd sell out his mother for a pack of smokes. No fucking way would he take a bullet or prison sentence for the men in the Brotherhood.

"The club bought a building on the outskirts of town. You and I need to clean it up. Get the trash out and make it ready for the contractors to look around."

"So, I'm a fucking janitor now?"

"More like a maid. I don't know why you're whining. I'm the one who already did all this grunt shit years ago to get my patch. Now, I have to do it again, just 'cause I spoke up for you."

JJ's frown fades when he hears I have his back. Loyalty to him is important. He expects to be treated well. Feels he deserves things because of who his father is, despite JJ having done nothing worth respecting.

"Everyone does the dirty shit in the beginning," I say, standing up. "Every fucking one except Mojo and Howler. Of course, they organized everything, which wasn't easy when the place used to be filled with moonshiners fucking goats in their front yards."

I throw down cash on the table for the waitress and think about what Hickory Creek was like back in the day. "This damn place was rough before the Brotherhood took control, and the Hallstead sisters stepped into the mayor and sheriff slots. Anyway, that's the past. These days, we got to earn our shit, so get up."

JJ moves with the urgency of a spoiled brat from the country club, thinking someone else should do the heavy lifting. Despite his attitude, I know being powerful men's sons doesn't mean anyone will hold our hands and help with the workload.

The sooner JJ realizes this fact, the sooner he'll freak out. Then, someone can finally put a bullet between his beady fucking eyes.

EIGHTEEN — HARMONY

Daisy and Ruby help me pick out my outfit based on the selfies I send. Keeping it simple, we choose a pink, lightweight skirt and a thin blue low-cut tank. To jazz it up, I wear heeled beige boots I bought from Goodwill a few months back.

My outfit looks sexy. My loose hair even behaves. I'm raring to go. Unfortunately, I manage this amazing feat about an hour before Dayton's arrival.

Until he shows up, I surf the internet and read about a strange sighting in London Harbor. A knock at the door rouses me from my focus on the unexplained.

I open the trailer door to find Dayton wearing a blue, buttoned-up shirt revealing more cleavage than my top does. I glance down at my low-cut shirt and wonder if I should change into something smuttier so I can compete with him.

"You look like an angel," he says in a weird, deep voice.

"What?"

"I'm saying you look hot."

"Thank you," I reply, reaching out to fix his shirt. "You look fancy. You know, for you."

Dayton pulls at his ponytail before yanking at his partially buttoned shirt. "Yeah, I figured I'd take you somewhere they require shoes. This shirt was in my closet, so I put it on."

Laughing, I step out of the trailer and pat his cheek. "Are you nervous?"

"No. Are you?"

"Of course not. I'm a grown woman capable of facing any situation."

"I bet you are. So, is the kid here?"

"Keanu is sleeping at Ruby's place. He misses his cousin."

"Then, your place is empty?"

"Yes, but you've got to earn your way inside," I explain while locking the door.

"You mean more than take you to a place that requires shoes?"

"Yeah, more than that, Dayton. You better charm me tonight if you want to get my panties off."

Taking my hand, he starts walking toward the parking lot. "How charming do I need to be if I'm willing to nail you while your panties are still on?"

"Same as if my panties come off. You need to be outstanding just to get into my trailer."

"What if I'm willing to do you on my Harley?" he asks while patting the bike's seat.

"I'm not screwing you in public."

"Even if I'm Hugh Grant level of charming?"

"Who?"

"That guy in those British romance movies."

"I don't watch British romance movies," I say, giving him a once-over. "To be honest, I'm less attracted to you now that I know you watch that crap."

"I don't watch them. My mom does."

"Sure," I say before sliding onto the Harley. "Did she pick out that shirt, too?"

When Dayton gives me a stubborn frown, I laugh again.

"I'm trying to be the guy you want."

"You don't know who that guy is if you think he watches Hugh Grant movies."

Dayton grunts like Daisy's cats do when they're ready to cough up a furball. I take his hand and guide it to my face.

"Is Hugh Grant a good kisser?" I whisper.

"How the fuck would I know?"

"Don't make me spell it out for you."

Dayton finally gives me a tiny smile. His lips cover mine, sending heat straight to the V between my legs. While he sucks deeply on my curious tongue, I stroke his face and enjoy the feel of his scruffy jaw against my fingertips.

"I thought about bringing a car," he says, once our lips part, "but the weather was too nice not to take the bike."

Wrapping my arms around his waist once he straddles the Harley, I sigh. "I agree."

The early summer heat feels good on my bare arms while we ride to The Eatery in the nearby town of White Horse. I don't need to ask why we can't eat somewhere closer. There's no privacy in Hickory Creek Township.

Once at The Eatery, we're seated in a curved booth in the back where it's too dark to see the food. I don't complain, though. This date isn't about our meal. I only want to know if Dayton and I can click in ways beyond amazing sex.

"Do you want to make chitchat while we wait for the food, or should we make out?" he asks after spreading his long, muscular arms along the booth's back.

"You've got to earn those kisses, Mister."

"What do you want to talk about?"

"Um, something easy, I guess. Like, what happened to Bryana?"

"Who?"

"The woman I fought with at Salty Peanuts."

"Oh, yeah, I don't know. The club girls smacked her around and likely kicked her out of the bar. Can't be sure since I never went back and asked them."

"Was JJ angry about what happened?"

"He's always angry. The guy has daddy *and* mommy issues. Chips on both shoulders. He's a mess," Dayton says and then adds, "He farts a lot, too. Just thought I'd mention that in case you were thinking about making a move for him."

"I already have my eye on another bad man, but thanks for the fart info."

Dayton smirks. "I do what I can to help out."

"I still can't believe I punched Bryana. I should control myself better."

"Yeah, you should. But she was a bitch, so who cares?"

"I do. I'm a mother and a professional who deals with temperamental patients. I can't slug people when they piss me off."

"That's different," Dayton says, taking my hand and stroking his leg with it. "Your kid isn't a bitch. And those people you work with are messed up in the head. It's not their fault they act like assholes. That chick, whatever her name was, she wants to piss people off. Well, part of pissing people off is accepting how sometimes you'll get punched. She learned that lesson. You did a good thing by schooling her ass."

"Yeah, but I expect more from myself."

"Fine, but I'm not helping you dump on your choices."

"I respect that."

Leaving my hand on his lap, Dayton plays with my hair as he scoots closer. "Tell me about that crypto crap you're into."

"I like reading about things that can't be currently explained."

"And you think it's real?"

"Most of it is, but maybe it's not what people think it is."

"You believe in ghosts?" he asks without laughing at me.

"Do you?"

"I don't know. I'd never thought about ghosts really."

"When I was a kid, we went with Mom's friend, Betty, to visit her family in Chattanooga. Her grandmother lived in an assisted living facility. It's the kind of place where a lot of people pass away. Then, while waiting for Betty, a chill brushed against me."

I graze Dayton's chest with my fingers so he can see how gentle the sensation felt.

"I wasn't near a window or a vent. The place was warm. I felt the chill a few times while we were there. Daisy and Mom felt it, too. Ruby was cranky and likely scared off the ghosts around her. That's why I believe in stuff we can't see."

"That's a neat story. How come you went with Betty to see her family?"

"You know why."

"Because your mom and Betty are *very close* friends?"

67

"Don't be a perv."

"Well, they *are* very close."

"Men have done them wrong, but their friendship endures. I wish I had a friend like that."

"You have your sisters."

"Yeah, and they have their men," I point out.

"Yeah, I'm forced to endure a bunch of gross PDA whenever I leave my condo. The other day, I got stuck in the elevator with my brother and Daisy. I thought they'd fuck right there. Talk about pervs."

Smiling, I pat his cheek, again enjoying the feel of his rough stubble.

"What are you thinking?" I ask when his dark gaze unsettles me.

"Tell me about the boy's father."

"Why won't you say Keanu's name?"

"It makes me think of him."

"Well, it is his name."

"No, it makes me think of his father. Tell me about the guy."

"I met Ji-Hoon at Tad's party. You know the one."

Dayton's gaze narrows. "Yeah, I know the one."

"You'd left, and I wasn't in the greatest mood. Everyone was getting on my nerves, and I was buzzed from drinking two screwdrivers. That's when Ji-Hoon came over and asked about my shirt."

"That Loch Ness one?"

"Yeah. He said he'd visited Scotland and saw the lake."

"You're telling me this guy traveled to Europe to see a lake where a monster was supposed to live?"

"No, he traveled there for work. Ji-Hoon had traveled all over for his work in technology sales. His dream trip was to visit the Congo to see where the Mokèlé-mbèmbé is reported to live."

"So, he was a nerd like you?"

"Wait, you think I'm a nerd?" I ask as my fingers play with a button on his shirt.

"Nerds can be sexy."

"Are you sure?" I whisper, sliding closer and pressing my side boob against his chest. "I would hate for you to slum it with a loser."

Dayton's smile turns predatory, sending a heatwave through my body. I feel it on my cheeks and pulsing between my legs. This man knows how to send my lust into overdrive. Though I can't strip away his power in the same way, I'm not without my talents.

Tonight, we'll find out which one of us has the upper hand.

NINETEEN — DAYTON

Harmony talks about her baby daddy with such ease. Her pale green eyes light up, and she smiles at the thought of him. If the guy weren't already a corpse, I'd need to dig him a grave. While it's not his fault he got to her before I did, I still resent his dead ass.

"So, you dropped your panties for a stranger just because he liked monsters?" I ask after our food arrives and Harmony inches away from me.

"Yes, that was exactly why. I'm glad you understand."

Grunting, I feel like an ape unable to form words. All I know is she's irritating me. Harmony ought to feel genuine shame about messing around with a guy who wasn't me. I mean, I felt bad for banging chicks who weren't her. *Fair is fair.*

"He wasn't in your league."

"Neither are you."

I study her, trying to figure out if she's messing with me. When Harmony only focuses on her chicken, I poke her shoulder.

"How so?"

"You've screwed everyone I know."

"Not everyone."

"So you say."

"I haven't screwed your sisters. Or your mom. Or Betty."

"Only because they wouldn't put out. If you thought you had a shot with them, you'd have taken it."

"That's how you see me, huh?"

Harmony glances at me and smiles. "That's how you see yourself. One time, you said you'd fuck anything with the right parts. You weren't choosy."

"I never said that."

"Did, too. We were at Red Barn. You'd downed a keg's worth of tequila to prove to me that you could drink a keg's

70

worth of tequila. I asked if you were going to die from alcohol poisoning. You said if you did die that you'd die happy since you'd already fucked all the women worth fucking. Then, you kept talking about fucking random women. I would have ditched you for being such a pig. Except I figured you might die. I didn't want you to be alone when the devil came knocking."

No way am I admitting to Harmony how I don't have any memories of that night. She's already too smug, and I'm still pissed about her putting out for another guy just because I bailed.

"I'm going to heaven, babe. Don't worry about that."

"You have the same look on your face as Keanu gets when I tell him it's almost bedtime."

"Why that guy?" I ask again, not finding her first answer satisfying.

"You weren't available."

"So, you wanted to punish me?"

"I didn't think you'd care. You left, remember?"

"So, then anyone would have gotten a shot?"

"No," she says, sitting back and sighing. "I wanted you, and you bailed. The other guys in this area bore me. They want to talk about how pretty I am or how my middle name is Tequila. They're loser versions of you. Then, Ji-Hoon came along, and he was different. I thought fate dropped a second chance in my lap. I'd get over you by spending time with a man nothing like you."

Her words kick me in the balls. I don't want her wanting anyone else. Not four years ago and not fucking now.

"If he had lived, would you be with him now?"

Harmony startles me by snorting before bursting into laughter.

"Yeah, can you imagine me living in South Korea away from my family? What a train wreck that would have been. Besides, Ji-Hoon's family would have freaked if he married a white woman. Heck, they weren't exactly thrilled to know he knocked up one."

"Are they shitty to you?"

71

"No," she says, and her expression softens. "They love Keanu. They talk to him online and send presents. They send money to help raise him, too. His mom says Keanu is all that's left of her son. They're good people. One day, I hope they can visit. In an ideal world, I could get the money to visit them when Keanu's old enough to deal with a long flight."

"Why couldn't Ji-Hoon move here with you if he lived?"

"We weren't in love, Dayton. We had a fling. After he left the US, we talked online about cryptozoology, not sex or being together. We were friends. He was sweet when I told him I was pregnant. He said he hoped our child had my smile. Yet, he never said anything about moving here or being with me. That was never an option for either of us. Stop acting as if he's my lost love, and you're my second choice."

"That's not how I'm acting."

"Bullshit. Now, eat your food before it gets cold."

Despite my bad mood, I laugh at how she sounds like my mom. That's the Harmony I dig. She says what she wants and does what she wants. I never need to worry about her lying to me. She doesn't see the point in faking anything.

"Is your food good?" I ask, cutting my steak.

As her gaze studies me, Harmony nods. She wonders if my mood will improve. I'm wondering that, too. Yet, I'm stuck thinking about the night I chose to walk away, and another guy swooped in.

Harmony might never have loved Ji-Hoon, but he created a child with her. A kid I'll look at for the rest of my life and see another man in his dark eyes.

Unlike Harmony, I believe in lying whenever necessary. People don't particularly like the truth most days anyway. Tonight, I give her a smile that promises her answers about Ji-Hoon have eased the angry male part of me. The lie improves the mood at dinner but fixes nothing I broke years ago.

TWENTY — HARMONY

Dayton eats his food like he's angry with it. He guts the steak and tears open the baked potato. Ramming bite after bite into his frowning mouth, he chews everything to a pulp before swallowing in a hard gulp.

Despite knowing why he's pissed, I chose to enjoy my meal. Dayton is stuck on a night long ago. Resentment glows in his dark eyes. Remaining silent, I can't think of a single thing to say. I'm here in the present, and I hold no regrets. To say I regret him not sleeping with me that night is to wish for a path that doesn't lead to Keanu in my life. Dayton is one delicious man, but my boy owns my heart.

"How come you never dated anyone after Ji-Hoon if he wasn't so special to you?" Dayton asks after punishing his meal.

"You're kidding, right?" I mutter, turning to face him in the booth before sitting cross-legged. "I had a baby."

"I know plenty of dating women with kids at home."

"So do I. But once Keanu was born, I found my new love." Shifting my arms into the position I used to cradle my baby, I continue, "I could look at his little face for hours. I was in awe of how I'd made someone so beautiful. Until Keanu, I'd only been a woman. Once he was born, I was a mother. No man could be as entertaining as my little guy."

"You still went out to Red Barn and enjoyed drinks."

"I needed time to decompress from work. Sometimes, my job can be depressing. You realize the people you're caring for will never improve. They're trapped in bodies and minds that won't cooperate. Often, they're in pain or full of frustration. When I was at the bar, people left me alone once you clarified how you thought I was your personal property. That meant I could drink and daydream and let my mind clear of all the negativity. Then I'd go home, feeling lighter and happier. It was better for Keanu and me, not to mention my clients who don't need more negativity in their lives."

73

"That's a lot of hippy-dippy thinking there."

"Not as much as the hippy-dippy thinking going on in here," I say, tapping my head. "Are you trying to say I'm a bad mom for wanting a few hours a month to decompress?"

"Don't put words in my mouth."

"Then, you put them in there and tell me what you mean."

Dayton leans his head back against the wall and sighs angrily. "I want you to tell me that you didn't date anyone after Ji-Hoon because you were waiting for me."

"I don't lie, and I wasn't waiting for you."

"Uh-huh."

"Were you waiting for me?"

"In a way."

"Well, I never thought we'd be together in a real way."

"We have chemistry."

"Yeah, but you bailed on me, and I had a baby. Chemistry or not, we're on different paths in life. I figured we'd hook up eventually. Then, you'd marry a tough biker lady. Meanwhile, I'd have unprotected sex with another random guy and give birth to his bastard. We'd all get what we needed and make sense."

"And you'd end up alone?"

"Oh, no, I fully plan to raise my kids to depend on me so much that they'll never leave. You know, like my mom did with me."

Dayton doesn't smile at my comment. In fact, his frown deepens. "So, the night I blew you off and the dead guy swooped in, you were looking to get knocked up?"

"Of course not. I was eighteen, but I'd never been good about remembering my birth control pills. They even have the days on them, but I'd think I took it in the morning when I actually took it the day before. Or a few days earlier. Things got blurred in my teenage brain. That's why I got an IUD after Keanu. No more worrying if I'll have a brain fart and forget a pill. Of course, I haven't needed it until the night with you. But then again, I figured that night would happen earlier."

"Then, why didn't it?"

74

"You tell me. I was always looking to make out and maybe more. Instead, you wanted to talk about the club or your brother or lately about your cousin, JJ. You were the one who put on the brakes."

"That I did. Except what's a man to do when he leaves a woman for a night, and she gets knocked up by some stranger?"

No way am I feeling guilty, even if that's what Dayton's hoping for. "Depends on what the man wants."

"He wants to go back in time and stop her from seeing anyone except him."

"Well, that's rather immature, don't you think? And one-sided. Especially since this man has seen every willing woman in their small town."

"That's an exaggeration."

"Well, it's *your* exaggeration."

"You don't like to lie, but I do it all the time. I say shit to make people think shit, but that doesn't mean shit is true."

Studying his unreadable expression, I have an incredible urge to hurry along our date. Dayton's being weird, but I need to push through my fears and force him into the truth.

"What's the point of lying about fucking everyone if it's not true?"

"The men in my club don't admire dick self-control. They'll never applaud a monogamous man. When Bonn went so long without sex, they thought he was weak. They admire men like my father and uncle who need fresh pussy like most people need to breathe."

"So, you lied because of peer pressure?"

"Why do you have to make it sound stupid?" he demands, seeming almost embarrassed.

"Because that's how it sounds to me. If anyone else told me they had to lie about their sex life to fit in with their friends, I'd think the same thing. Don't be so sensitive."

"Fuck that. If you don't get by this point how everything you say is personal to me, then I don't know how to make it clearer."

I again study Dayton's expression, seeing past his cranky exterior. "We do have chemistry. You've got to wonder what would happen if you could feel this chemistry with someone better suited for your lifestyle."

"I can't think of another woman when you're sitting so close."

"Perhaps, if you get me out of your system, you can find a woman better fitted for your life."

"Shut up."

"You shut up," I snap, falling into my role as the baby of the family by demanding to be heard.

"I'm not the one talking about me finding another woman."

"Do you want to know what I think?"

"Probably not."

"I think I remind you of your mom, and that's why you have a hard-on for me."

Shaking his head, Dayton gives me a dirty look. "Don't think talking about my mom and getting hard for you will keep me from wanting to fuck you."

"Why would I want to get out of sex when that's all I want you for?"

Dayton narrows his eyes and glares nasty at me, but I only smile. Leaning forward, I pucker up and dare him not to kiss me. His lust overpowers his ego, forcing his lips to cover mine.

As weak as I make him, I don't trick myself into thinking his desire and possessiveness mean he's in it for the long haul. Dayton wants me to be his, so he can know he won a contest taking place only in his beautiful head.

TWENTY-ONE — DAYTON

Harmony tastes like honey mustard sauce and fuck-me promises. I wrap my arm around her waist, tugging her body against mine. We're in a packed restaurant but might as well be alone. I don't see or want anyone else. To make Harmony mine, I'm willing to walk through fire, cut loose all my ties, and fall to my knees to beg.

Except she isn't playing fair.

"Let me ask you something," I say with my lips an inch from hers. "Didn't you think about how hooking up with a stranger like Ji-Hoon might lead to you giving your kid a fatherless upbringing like you had?"

"Yes, I totally thought about that. But he was so sexy that I just couldn't help myself."

Harmony's icy gaze holds mine. This woman won't be poked without taking a swipe back. Best of all, she does the entire thing with a smile.

"Do you ever think about your dead daddy?"

"No, and Ji-Hoon didn't remind me of him, either. My father was a blond ski bum who died of alcohol poisoning. Ji-Hoon was an educated dark-haired professional who was hit by a taxi by no fault of his own. If anything, you remind me of my dead daddy, Jan."

Sighing, I lean my head against the wall. "I don't want to play anymore."

Harmony pats my thigh. "Why are you asking me all these questions about Ji-Hoon and now my father?"

"I want you to feel guilty for cheating on me, even though we weren't together."

"Okay, but I do feel guilty. I should have waited for you. If I could go back to that night, I would blow off Ji-Hoon and never get pregnant. Then, I'd be pure for you when you finally worked up the courage to fuck me stupid. Do you feel better now?"

"Yeah, actually," I mutter, sliding her hand from my thigh to the erection I've endured for an hour.

"When was the last time you were with a woman who wasn't me?"

"I don't know."

Harmony strokes my erection through my jeans before squeezing it threateningly. "Yes, you do."

"Last night."

"Try again."

"An hour before I picked you up."

"One more time."

"Two years ago, after I saw you walking with your boy. I'd been pissed at you for not waiting. But you looked too good that day. I knew no other woman was good enough for my dick again."

Harmony stares at me, wondering if I'm lying again. Even unsure, her hand never stops stroking me. The woman has me nearly ready to jizz in my pants at a family restaurant.

"You're not a good man," she whispers. "But you're not all bad, either."

I know her words mean she's opening herself to me. Yet, I can't think of anything except the building pressure in my balls. Resting my head back on the wall again, I close my eyes and try to look like a man chilling and not one about to come.

Harmony doesn't relent, even after I grit my teeth to keep from groaning. She strokes me long after I've emptied myself into a conspicuous spot on my jeans.

"Think anyone will notice?" I ask, opening my eyes.

"Do you care if they do?"

"No, but I figured you might."

"People think I'm trailer trash. They claim my kid is a half-breed bastard. They call my clients horrible names and think they'd rather die than end up like them. People don't impress me, so I don't give even the tiniest shit about impressing them."

Taking her hand from my now relaxed cock, I hold it against my chest. "You're worth waiting for, but I need to fuck you tonight. I don't care where or how, but I need to shove my cock as deep inside you as you can handle. I need to pound you until you beg me to stop. Then, I need to pound you a bit more. And every time I can't keep from bending you over, that's on you, Harmony Tequila Slater. You did this to me, and you need to help me deal with the consequences."

"Pay the check," she says, giving me a sly grin. "Then, drive me to my trailer and bend me over. I want to see how much of a bite comes with that bark of yours."

Without looking away from Harmony's still smiling face, I wave the waitress over and ask for the check. I pay and leave a nice tip since my woman keeps track of things like that.

When we stand, I maneuver her in front of me to hide the wet spot. But she wiggles free, stands next to me proudly, and takes my hand. Harmony's fearless right now, and I doubt she's ever looked as beautiful.

TWENTY-TWO — HARMONY

Dayton devours my lips as soon as I shut my trailer door. I struggle to hold him back. Should we talk more? Maybe he can say something romantic again like that waiting for me thing. The ride home reminds me of who he is and who I am, and how I'm completely out of my league with this man's lifestyle.

But I tell myself this is just sex. We still have time to work on the details and figure out how a man like Dayton fits in a life like mine. I certainly don't fit in his.

Sex makes sense, though. We don't need to worry about kids or jobs. No past or future. I can shut off my brain for a few hours and forget about everything besides the man stripping out of his clothes.

"I'm going to fuck you raw," he growls, kicking off his shoes and dropping his pants.

I don't pay attention to his words. I'm too busy enjoying the exquisite view of Dayton Rutgers buck naked. My gaze devours the sight of him in the way his lips claimed me earlier.

"Now you," he demands, sounding as angry as his erect cock looks.

"I'm too shy. Let me undress in the dark."

Laughing before I finish saying the words, I run toward my bedroom. Dayton follows, stomping and exhaling like a pissed bull.

No! He's Big Foot coming to ravage an innocent camper. Just the thought sends my giggles into overdrive until I can barely breathe, let alone remove my sandals.

Dayton grabs my ankle as I sit on the floor. He lifts my foot and unsnaps my strap. "It's all fun and games until someone gets fucked senseless."

I lift my other sandal for him to remove. His gaze focuses on my parted legs, now bare from my skirt sliding to my waist.

80

"You're Sasquatch," I gasp, trying not to laugh. "A ferocious animal."

"Get your panties off."

"You take them off, beast man."

Dayton frowns at my giggling but doesn't hesitate to reach down and drag my panties off my hips and down my legs. He presses the pink fabric to his nose.

"You smell wet. Are you ready to be fucked?"

"Yes, you big scary monster man."

"Are you drunk?"

Sitting up, I tug off my shirt and pop off my bra. "Have you ever seen a human woman's breasts before?"

"You are drunk," he says, reaching out to pinch my right nipple.

My hand strokes his thick cock as I lift my gaze to meet his. "I'm a virgin hiker in the woods, and you're a big, hairy beast with a raging hard-on." Letting go of him, I turn around and wiggle my ass. "Please be gentle, beast man."

When Dayton says nothing, I worry he might pull some bullshit about not wanting to play. Instead, he leans forward and bites my left ass cheek. I yelp in surprise and pain. Glancing back at him, I find him sniffing me.

"This is your pussy," he growls, spreading my flesh open with his fingers. "It can fit me. No, I will make it fit. I want to fuck, and you can't escape."

Dayton reaches over and grabs my hair, fisting it roughly. I bite my lower lip and smile as his cock probes my wet flesh.

"I'm scared," I mumble, trembling despite my grin.

"You should be."

Dayton shoves his cock into me in a violent, painful thrust. My gasp comes out as a pained squeak, and I feel him falter.

"I was a virgin, you bad, bad beast."

Exhaling hard, Dayton tugs roughly at my hair, twisting my head back so he can lick my lips.

"Should we have a safe word?" he whispers in my ear.

"How about 'knock that off, you stupid fucker' or something obvious like that?"

Dayton grins while his free hand reaches under me and pinches my nipples. First, the left and then the right. He doesn't move his hips, leaving his cock shoved as deep into me as my body will allow.

His lips suck at the soft skin on my shoulders before his teeth nip at my throat. He inhales my scent deeply, and then his hips begin to move. He thrusts his cock into me, and I can't escape. One hand fists my hair and keeps my head tilted back. The other grips my left tit, pinching the nipple between his unyielding fingers.

"Too hard," I whimper, wanting more.

"Not hard enough."

Dayton drives his cock into me with more force. His hands tighten their grip too. I can't believe how rough he's being and how much better it feels than I fantasized.

I hear him grunt with every thrust. His balls slap against my pussy, teasing my swollen clit. I want more. I want him to fuck me until I'm a shivering, satisfied mess.

"Please stop," I beg, shoving my ass and seeking more cock.

"Shut up."

Dayton releases my tit and then shoves two of his fingers into my mouth.

"Suck it," he demands, nearly yelling.

My mouth closes on his fingers, sucking hungrily, wanting to show how I'll pleasure him next. When I imagine I'm sucking his cock, my pussy throbs with excitement.

Once I've slathered his fingers with spit, he yanks his hand away and returns it to my tits. I moan at the feel of his wet fingers twisting my nipple. He roughly kneads them at the same tempo as his driving hips pump into me.

"I'm going to jizz in you. Fill you with my seed. Make you my whore."

"Oh," is all I can moan as the pleasure builds.

Though I'm so close, I don't know if I can push over the edge before he does. Fucking with more intensity, we're suddenly in a race to see who can come first. I know he's closer to finishing. His breathing is faster, harsher, and I'm still not there.

Reaching between my legs, I would have fallen forward if Dayton wasn't holding me still by my hair. My fingers find my clit and the hot flesh of his balls. I don't know which one to touch. I'm tempted to enjoy his heavy sac, and I'm dying to know how it tastes.

But this is a race, and Dayton is about to pass the finish line. My frenzied fingers caress my clit, wanting to come and feel the pleasure to go with all this delicious pain. *I'm so close...*

Grunting, Dayton shoves his cock deep inside me while his balls let loose. The thought of him filling me with his jizz provides me the extra mental stimulation I need to find my climax.

I howl like a wounded animal, reaching the most intense pleasure I've ever experienced. Dayton pumps into me, insisting I take more of him and making me come harder. He's unhinged behind me. I both laugh and cry at how our bodies aren't satisfied even after such intensity.

Even when his dick softens, Dayton won't stop fucking me. He shoves my face into the mattress and holds me still while struggling to remain deep in my pussy.

"I want to come again," I beg. "Finger me. Eat me out. Play with my clit. Just make me come."

Dayton's cock finally leaves my tender pussy, only to be replaced by two fingers. They mercilessly pump into me, and I whine from the building pleasure.

"Tease your clit," he demands, keeping my head pinned to the mattress. "Show me how you like it."

I reach between my legs and give my swollen nub what it craves. Making fast, rough circles, my fingers work with his until my pussy clenches and my body trembles from another climax.

Dayton pumps his fingers until I nearly collapse on the bed. Leaning over, he licks my ear.

"Good thing you got lost in the woods, young lady. I can't imagine what I'd do with all this cum otherwise."

Smiling at his tone, I enjoy the feel of his now raging hard cock taunting my clit.

"Keep your face down and your ass up."

"Please don't hurt me anymore."

Dayton slaps my ass, making me jump. I haven't finished squealing when his cock returns to where it belongs. Soon, we embark on another rough, wild adventure.

TWENTY-THREE — DAYTON

I never would have guessed Harmony Slater was a kinky minx. Our first time was fast and rough because we were drunk. I also hadn't stuck my dick in a woman in years. That night, I was just lucky I didn't jizz the minute my cock came within an inch of her pussy.

Tonight, when Harmony comes so hard from our rough fucking, I wonder if I can get her off any other way.

By the time I let her roll over and rest on her back, she looks spent. I even worry I was too rough despite her amazing orgasms.

"I admit I read Big Foot erotica a few years back," she says when I relax on my side next to her. "Something about the way you were breathing and grunting made it all come back."

Harmony sounds embarrassed by her fantasies. I remain silent, just enjoying how good my well-used cock feels after too long with only my hand.

My fingers caress her throat before sliding down between her perky tits. After circling each hard nipple, I explore her stomach. Finally, my fingers dip between her legs, where her soft blonde hairs remain drenched in our fluids.

"You smell good," I say, lifting my fingers to lick the juices from them. "I never thought pussy smelled so good, but yours is like perfume."

Harmony watches me explore until I spread her pussy open and look at her pink clit. Exhaling softly, she closes her eyes and opens her legs wider. I lick my finger and run the tip over her swollen flesh.

"A lot of girls can't get off," I say in a soft, almost menacing voice. "But all you need is this little button in your pussy to be pushed just right."

I make faster circles around the flesh, which swells even more, almost begging to be sucked.

"I've never wanted to taste a clit before. Is it like candy?"

Harmony's mouth opens, and she breathes faster as I twist around on the bed. I watch her tits rise and fall faster with her increased breathing. I'll suck her pink nipples soon. But for now, my mouth waters at the thought of her fat little prick.

Her bed feels too small for my body, but I maneuver onto all fours, so my face is over her waiting cunt. Harmony immediately takes my cock, stroking it.

"Not yet," I say, removing her hand. "I need to focus on your pussy. You can play with my cock when I'm done."

Harmony swallows hard. Her pussy clenches as my fingers tease the other flesh.

"Do you want me to lick it?" I ask.

"Yes."

"How bad do you want it?"

"Please, Dayton."

"Promise no other man can suck this clit."

"No one else. I promise."

"Did Ji-Hoon suck it?"

"You know he didn't. There's only you. Please, Dayton."

Smiling at how she begs, I lower my face until her scent overwhelms me. My dick is painfully hard now, but I need to taste her before finding relief.

Her pussy clenches when I give her clit even the tiniest lick. A second taste makes Harmony moan. I want to be gentle, just to know if I can make her come without having to flick this tender flesh.

That said, her orgasm needs to happen quickly now that my dick is too painful to ignore. The damn thing is already leaking in Harmony's hand now that she's stroking me again.

My tongue finds a tender yet unrelenting rhythm she replicates with her hand. Harmony takes less licking than I do stroking. Her orgasm washes over her, leaving her body covered in goose bumps. I don't remove my tongue until her arched back settles onto the mattress and her breathing slows.

Turning on the bed, I cover her mouth with mine. Harmony sucks gently at my tongue, and her fingers stroke my face. I don't release her lips while my body adjusts on the bed, so I'm between her legs. Harmony lifts her hips, searching for my cock. I press it against her flesh and ease inside her. For this fuck, I plan to take my time, so Harmony will need to be patient.

When my lips finally leave hers, Harmony's gaze locks on my face and watches me intently while I prop myself over her body. I move slowly, allowing every inch of my cock to savor the heat of her wet pussy. Harmony doesn't reach for her clit or tits. She doesn't rush for an orgasm. Her only focus is my face. I feel exposed with her staring at me in this way, but I love the rawness of her gaze.

No barriers remain between us. Harmony sees into me down to my core, and she can't look away.

I don't think there's a more powerful feeling than knowing my woman accepts me. Nothing and no one can defeat me. I'm a fucking powerhouse, ready to destroy any obstacle standing in my way. All because of this beautiful woman and her ability to see past my bullshit to the man I hide underneath.

TWENTY-FOUR — HARMONY

Waking up next to Dayton, I can't feel my legs. After a struggle, I lift myself up on my elbows and look at the nearby clock. The sun seems brighter than it should at eight in the morning. I consider returning to sleep, but Keanu is waiting for me to pick him up at Ruby's.

I roll to my side and force my jelly legs to hold me up for the trip to the bathroom. Taking cautious steps, I worry my vagina will fall into the toilet.

Just the thought of such a thing sends me into giggles. Though I've tried remaining nonchalant about sex, there's so much I didn't know. Like how it feels for a man to literally fuck my brains out. I mean, I doubt I could perform even basic math right now and forget about spelling anything correctly.

Still naked on the toilet, I reach over to start the shower. I wish I had my phone so I could check for messages. Too tired to walk back to my room just feet away, I remain seated until the water gets hot.

A few minutes after stumbling under the shower, I shuffle back out and search for a towel. Still damp, I return to the bedroom and fight the urge to snuggle next to Dayton for a few hours.

"Why do you get up so early?" Dayton asks, hiding his eyes under his arm.

"I need to pick up Keanu."

Dayton's fingers caress my back while I search my dresser for clothes.

"It's hot in your place."

"Summer will do that," I mumble, pulling up my panties and a loose skirt. "I had fun last night."

"I know you did. I was there for all the moaning."

I glance at him over my shoulder. "You surprise me. I'd think a man with your wealth, power, and good looks wouldn't be so insecure."

Dayton narrows his eyes and gives me a smirk. "You're feisty in the morning. Let's take a ride on the Dayton Dick Train."

"No, thank you. I already put on my bra. Once that happens, the party is over."

I stand and tug on my yellow "Frankie Says Relax" shirt. Turning to face Dayton, I find him stretched out with a raging hard-on.

"You'll need to handle that on your own."

"That's been the story of my life for the last two years."

Smiling, I throw his jeans over his legs. "Get dressed."

"Did you at least make coffee?"

"No," I say and walk out of the room. "If I had fresh coffee, I'd want to chill. There's no time for that. I need to pick up Keanu and grab a few groceries. Then, I can nap."

"So, you're saying," Dayton mutters while appearing from the bedroom wearing his jeans, "I should come over later if I want to cuddle."

"If you come over, just know Keanu will be here, and we'll be clothed for all cuddling."

A smiling Dayton wraps an arm around my shoulders. "You're so stuck on me. Poor thing."

"Where's your shirt?" I ask, right before he kisses me.

Popping his lips free, Dayton shrugs. "I don't know. You ravaged me hard last night. I wouldn't be surprised if you shredded it."

I dodge his next kiss and walk to the bedroom, where I find his boxers and shirt.

"You skipped a step," I point out while throwing the boxers at him.

"My dick likes the rough stuff, but you already knew that."

Giggling despite my fatigue, I slide on my sandals and kick his boots toward him.

"I've got to go."

"So, I'll follow you over to make sure no one hassles you."

"Like that would happen."

Dayton shoves his feet into his boots and yanks at the ties. "Never know. This area is in flux."

Once he's dressed, we leave the trailer and head to the parking lot where he rides his Harley, and I drive my compact car. The entire trek across town to his condo, he flirts with me. Pulling up to my window to wink or tug at his dick, the man has sex on his mind.

When we arrive at the condos, Dayton kisses me from my car into the elevator and then to Ruby's door.

"So, we can hook up next Friday, if you want," I say, unaccustomed to after date/sex chit chat.

"Nope. I'll probably drop by your place whenever I want. Might sleep over."

"Or we can hook up next Friday."

Dayton pins me between his body and the wall. "If you run, I will chase you. If you hide, I will find you. If you tell me no, I will stalk you into a yes. No matter what, you're not shaking me loose."

"Oh, I'll shake you loose just fine if I want," I say, poking his chest. "I'll do whatever I want, mister."

Smiling, he kisses my forehead. "Sorry for the morning breath."

"I've tasted worse."

"No, you haven't," he says, instantly wearing a jealous frown.

"How about the first time we hooked up? You were sporting some serious mouth stink that morning."

Smiling again, Dayton backs up so I can get to Ruby's door. "I'll be looking for you soon."

"Okay, but maybe give my vagina a few days to recover."

"Is that a real request?"

Nodding, I knock on Ruby's door. Dayton gives me a smirk to end all smirks.

"Poor Harmony and her poor vagina."

Sharing his grin, I only look away when Ruby answers. I hear Keanu running on the hardwood floors. The only guy who can make me smile more than the sexy jerk I spent the night with is the sweet little boy barreling toward me now.

90

Once I'm inside the condo, Ruby peeks out into the hall to give Dayton a smile.

"Keep walking, stud."

"Stop flirting," I hear Dayton say. "What would Bonn think?"

Laughing, Ruby shuts the door. Turning to me, she shakes her head.

"On the first date? Where's your self-control?"

"Probably wherever I stashed my self-respect," I say, picking up Keanu. "Did you miss me?"

Keanu nods and shows Carl to me. "We slept in Elle's bed."

"Did you sleep well?"

"It's a big bed."

Smiling, I cuddle him tighter against me. He hugs me back for nearly a minute before wanting his freedom. Squirming, he gets me to put him on the floor.

"Can I play?"

"Yep."

Keanu runs back to where his cousin sits on the floor with her dolls.

"Was he good last night?"

"Perfect," Ruby says, handing me a cup of coffee. "Don't be upset, but he talked to Hayes's kids."

Angus Hayes is the big boss in the town of White Horse. Nothing about him is friendly, and I can't imagine why his kids would be talking to mine.

"How?"

"Skype. Elle chats with them every day. Mostly, they talk about how school is lame and what they'll do if the zombies come. They're very into preparing for the end of the world. I'm sure they get that from Hayes."

"Why would they want to talk to a three-year-old? Aren't they fifth graders?"

"He's Elle's cousin, and they're pretty attached to her."

"Huh."

"They feel like outsiders. Elle does, too. Makes sense even if Hayes creeps me out."

"He doesn't creep me out. He's just a man."

"So tough," she teases, poking me. "How was your date?"

I sit on a stool at the kitchen island. "Pretty excellent. He asked me many questions that he's clearly been thinking about for a long time. He also gave me some crap that I threw back at him. In the end, he claimed to have been waiting for me for two years."

"Waiting?"

"Sex wise."

"No way."

"I believe him, but I'm a sap who believes everyone."

Ruby leans against the counter. "I've heard of his many conquests. Hard to believe they were all wrong."

Shrugging, I feel a little defensive. "I'll believe Dayton until someone proves him a liar."

Ruby narrows her gaze and points at me. "You know, all those times I heard about him partying and fucking chicks, no one ever said who the chicks were. I mean, I never asked or cared because his dick wasn't my problem. I assumed they were club sluts that got passed around. Hmm, I wonder if anyone would even notice if he actually stopped fucking chicks and just acted like he was."

"Clearly, they didn't," I say, holding onto my belief in Dayton.

"He's a tricky shit, ain't he?"

"That he is."

"Well, good for him. Two years is plenty of time to check out his dick to make sure it's squeaky clean for you."

"Is there anyone more romantic than you?"

Smiling, Ruby shrugs. "I had an entire speech ready for why Dayton was bad news, but if he really has been waiting, my plan is a flop."

"Thank goodness. I'm too tired for speeches."

Ruby gives me a wink. "I bet you are. Let's just hope Dayton isn't as bad an influence on you as Camden is with Daisy. She probably won't be up until after noon today."

"Let her enjoy her childless fun. Soon, she'll be up early like the rest of us."

Ruby nods knowingly before her gaze leaves me and focuses on Bonn appearing from the bedroom. Clearly, just out of the shower, he buttons his shirt and looks ready to go.

"Where are you off to?" I ask.

"Work. Need to run around and spy on people. Then, I'll be home to take my girls out for dinner. Want to come along?"

I look at my sister, finding her smiling casually at me. I see past her ruse and know she'd rather have alone time with her soon-to-be husband and their daughter. While Keanu and I are welcome to come along, we'll be a third wheel.

"I'll let Keanu play a bit longer. Then, we need to do errands, and I'd like to veg tonight."

Ruby smiles wider, knowing I caught onto her silent begging. Watching us give each other signals, Bonn likely wonders if he would be as obnoxious with his siblings if he'd grown up with any. I suspect he would if Dayton and Camden are any indication of how brothers act.

TWENTY-FIVE — DAYTON

Waking up before noon ought to be a sin. Yeah, the rest of the world can do what it wants, but so much sunshine so early in the day feels evil to me. I force my tired ass out of bed anyway. Going through the motions of working out and picking up a late breakfast at IHOP, I don't really wake up until around two.

At that point, my day becomes a waiting game.

JJ texts me a few times, wanting to meet up and get a beer. I tell him I've got shit to do for my mom. Not long after I blow off JJ, Camden wants me to head to Salty Peanuts for a beer. I tell him I'm on my way to the clinic to check my dick for infections. That excuse gets him off my back.

Now, I'm back to waiting for Harmony to leave work. I need a reminder she's worth all the turmoil I suffer. In my heart, I know she's my sunshine, so bright and powerful. But when she's gone from my sight too long, I start doubting her charming smile or the way she never flinches, even when I stare greedily at her.

Harmony's shift at the group home ends at three. By four, she'll be home and ready to entertain the man of her dreams. *That's what I tell myself, anyway.*

I arrive at Lush Gardens ten minutes to four, having waited as long as I can. Before reaching her trailer, I hear Harmony's voice, along with the sound of splashing water.

Turning the corner, I find Keanu stomping in a small plastic pool. The kid is wearing a swimsuit and his bucket hat. Sitting on an old folding chair, Harmony is a temptress wearing only a blue and white striped bikini bottom and an oversized white tank. Her long hair dips into the pool when she leans forward to flick water at Keanu's legs.

"Nice swimsuit," I say, squatting next to the pool. "You like dinosaurs, huh?"

Keanu stops stomping and points at the T-Rex on his swim trunks. "Grr," he says and then smiles at his mother before kicking his feet in the water again.

"We just got this at Wal-Mart," Harmony explains, fixing the tie on the front. "Isn't he adorable?"

I nod, but my gaze feasts on Harmony's bare flesh. "Are you sure you should be dressed like that?"

"Why wouldn't I?"

"You shouldn't advertise all your gifts to the world."

"As an unmarried woman on the prowl for a man, doesn't advertising make sense?"

Now, I'm the one who growls. Harmony laughs and claps her hands. Keanu immediately claps his hands, too. He stomps faster, spraying water far enough to reach my pant leg. His dark eyes wait to see if I'm mad. When I don't say anything, he smiles at his mom.

"Did you come here for a specific reason?" Harmony asks.

"I wanted to see you and figured you'd be home from work by now."

"You weren't wrong," she says, patting my jaw with her wet fingers.

"If he weren't in that pool, I'd dunk you right now. Then, I'd do other stuff I shouldn't say."

"You can stay over tonight," Harmony says, holding my gaze. "Only if you promise to behave, though."

Keanu points at the sky and yells, "Plane!" like it's the most impressive thing ever. He then checks to see if Harmony also sees it. The way he craves her approval reminds me of that handsome guy I see in the mirror every day.

"I can pick up dinner from somewhere," I offer.

"That's okay."

"You wouldn't have to cook."

Harmony considers my offer. "I don't want you thinking I keep you around to pay for things. With that said, I can't afford food out tonight, so you'd have to pay. Decisions, decisions."

"Sweet, naïve, Harmony, there you go again with your silly thinking. We both know why you keep me around, and it has nothing to do with what's in my pockets. Though it has *everything* to do with what's in my pants."

She gives me a wide smile before returning to flicking water at Keanu. The kid is talking to the toy in his hand, and I can't understand a single word he's saying. I wouldn't be surprised if he were speaking a foreign language.

Somehow, Harmony deciphers his babble and coos approvingly about whatever the hell he's talking about. My gaze flashes from them to her bare leg only inches from where I've taken a seat in another folding chair. Her golden skin shines in the sunlight, and I can't keep my fingers from caressing what my eyes feast on.

Harmony ignores my hand, but I don't doubt her body knows what I offer. Leaning over, I peek into her tank to find bare breasts and hard pink nipples. *Oh, her body is very aware of what my fingers promise if we can just get alone.*

"What kind of food would you pick up for dinner?" she asks without looking at me.

"Anything you want."

Her smile is only interrupted by a quick lick of her lips. I don't need her to spell things out. This is how mommies and daddies work out sex deals in front of the kids. I figure it's what my parents did and what Bonn and Ruby do every night.

Now, I'm playing a family man with a woman anyone would feel lucky to claim as his.

TWENTY-SIX — HARMONY

Keanu splashes in the pool for another hour, telling Carl a story about police and firemen fighting dinosaurs. Loving his tales, I reach into my bag and grab my phone. I videotape Keanu, so overwhelmed with mama pride that I nearly forget the sexy bad man fondling my leg.

Dayton remains patient while Keanu plays. He doesn't check his phone or sigh with boredom. Instead, he asks me questions about Keanu's likes and dislikes. He genuinely seems interested in my kid and our life. *Damn, if he isn't making me fall for him even harder.*

"Enjoying the pool?" Charlie asks, walking over to us while taking her little dog for a walk.

"It's hot inside, and Keanu loves the water."

My baby throws his arms in the air and announces, "I'm a fish!"

Charlie and I laugh at his enthusiasm while Dayton grins. I suspect my mom's best buddy is checking to make sure the scary biker man isn't causing trouble. Her neighborly visit backfires when Dayton sees an opportunity.

"Charlie, you're good with kids," Dayton says, standing up.

"I hope so since I watch them for a living. That's a fact you already knew, though. So, what's your point?"

"Could you watch the little man for a few minutes while I work out some issues with his mama?"

Charlie looks at me, and I must seem worried because she quickly agrees.

Of course, I'm mostly embarrassed because I know exactly what Dayton needs to work out with me.

He walks inside as Charlie sits in the chair he vacated. I tell Keanu I'll be back in a few minutes.

Once inside, I quietly latch the door lock and walk to the couch. With his jeans around his ankles, Dayton fists his erect cock.

"I need your pussy."

"I'll suck you off," I say, nervous about Keanu and Charlie just outside.

"No, I've been thinking about that bikini bottom being the only damn thing keeping me from looking at your pussy. I've got to fuck it."

Glancing back at the door, I whisper, "I get loud."

"I'll cover your mouth. Gag you if necessary."

Before I can complain, Dayton kisses me hard. I reach down and stroke his cock. With his hands free, he removes my shirt and pinches my hard nipples.

"You've been teasing me with these bitches. You know I want to suck them," Dayton says, sitting on the couch and tugging me closer so he can latch onto my right nipple.

"Oh," I sigh while still stroking his cock.

Dayton forces me to rest my hands on his shoulders. He says nothing before sucking at the left nipple. My pussy clenches at the pleasure of his lips plucking at my hard flesh.

"Oh, Dayton," I moan in a hushed voice.

Startling me, he bites my nipple hard before suddenly letting it go. His hands grip my hips, forcing me to turn around. His fingers reach between my legs and shove the bikini bottom aside.

I try not to gasp when he leans me back, so my legs are on the outside of his. He then lowers my pussy onto his waiting cock.

"Let me fuck you."

"We have to be quiet."

Dayton responds by covering my mouth with his right hand. His left one dips between my legs and gives my clit a fast slap. I flinch on his lap while my pussy can't stop sucking his cock. Despite my fear of getting caught, I ache to be fucked by this man.

His hips drill upward, sending his cock deeper into me. I'm a wet noodle against him. No power to stop what's happening. I can't speak with his hand covering my mouth. I can't work his cock out of me. I can't swat away his fingers taunting my swollen clit. I can only rest against his hard body and let him fuck me until he's finished.

Moaning against his palm, I love how roughly he plays with my clit. His fingers slap it, followed by a cruel little pinch. My whimpers and moans get muffled by his hand pressed tightly against my lips.

Through all the brutal teasing of my clit, Dayton never slows his hips. They thrust up, shoving his cock deeper into my body. He opens my pussy until my flesh is merely an extension of his.

I imagine how I look. Legs spread wide open. Bright red pussy slapped and fucked into submission. Hard nipples jut from my bouncing tits. I'm the picture of a woman completely under the power of this man's lust.

Coming blindingly hard, I close my eyes and enjoy the images in my head. Dayton Rutgers is a fucking machine, and I'm at the mercy of his powerful hips and thick cock.

"You need to come again before I jizz in you. Your boy's waiting," he mocks. "Tell your pussy to hurry up."

I hear humor in his voice, but we both know how much we're not ready for this to end. The world is just outside, going on as if we're not rutting like animals only feet away. I should care. Yet, right now, I can only think about how lucky I am to have Dayton inside me.

I do come, and I come hard. Jerking wildly in his grip, I moan like a horny cat behind his hand. Dayton chuckles against my cheek when he hears me orgasm. I want to kiss him so badly, but his hand remains over my mouth until he's come inside me.

"Every drop," he says, pumping up into my body. "Make your pussy swallow it all."

My body sucks at his cock, wanting his seed to stay inside.

"I pounded your pussy something fierce," he says, sliding his hand from my mouth so he can kiss me.

For the next few minutes, his hips pump into me leisurely. I suck at his tongue with the same soft hunger as my pussy does his cock. His fingers play with my nipples, and I can imagine us going to the bedroom where he might fuck me again. Or I could suck him. Or he could eat me out.

I can think of so many pleasurable activities we could do if we were alone.

But we're not.

As magical as my life might be if I did nothing more than bend over for this man, I'm a mother with responsibilities.

Standing, I struggle against my wobbly legs. Dayton steadies me before he shoves his well-fucked cock in his jeans. I look around for my shirt and readjust my bikini bottom. Once I'm dressed, I glance at a casual Dayton.

"How do I look?"

"Like you just got fucked by a giant cock."

I walk into the bathroom to splash water on my face. While my cheeks remain rosy, the trailer isn't air-conditioned, and the temperature hit 80 today.

Dayton is standing near the door when I leave the bathroom.

"Are you still staying now that you got laid?" I ask, fanning my cheeks.

"Don't be cold after you've ravaged my body for your needs," he teases and leans over to kiss my forehead. "I want to be anywhere you are. Besides, one fuck does not satisfy a man who's waited so long for his special pussy."

Rolling my eyes, I pretend I'm not relieved to know he'll stay for dinner. I refuse to let Dayton have all the power. However, I feel like I'm falling too fast and hard to be healthy. This sexy man talks a good game about waiting for me, and I'm desperate to believe his every word.

Too bad I know he lies, especially to himself.

TWENTY-SEVEN — DAYTON

Harmony's trailer is too fucking small. I try to relax on her couch, but it's more like a loveseat. Feeling cramped, I stand in the living room and survey the tiny open area. The kitchen fits Harmony and the kid fine, and they move around easily. Meanwhile, I smack my elbow on the fridge and then my knee against the dark blue island-style cart.

"The food will be here soon," Harmony says while running her fingers down my back. "I hope you like it."

"If I don't, I'll order pizza. I remember you saying you like leftovers."

"Leftovers!" Keanu yells, jumping around the living room with his LEGO man in one hand and a small plastic airplane in the other.

"Are you okay?" Harmony asks when I can't find a place to stand.

"Your trailer is tiny."

"I know, but it's only Keanu and me."

"Do you like it being so small?"

"If I had the money, I'd get something bigger."

"How come Daisy's place never seemed so small? Or Ruby's?"

"Daisy has cats, so her place isn't filled with toys. Same with Ruby since Elle is past her little kid toy phase."

"Small humans need space, I guess."

"I'm sorry if you're not comfortable here," she says, wrapping her arms around my waist.

"Are you really?"

"Yes."

"Are you sure because you sounded sarcastic when you said it?"

"Look, I want you to be comfortable. However, I won't apologize for living modestly on the salary I get from a job I love."

"What about the money the kid's grandparents send?"

101

"I told you how I save half each month for emergencies or stuff he'll need when he gets older. Like braces or college. I want to be smart with money."

"I want you to have nice things," I say, scratching the back of my neck. "I'm fairly sure my way is right."

"Fairly sure or not, you're still wrong. Now, settle down, find a place to sit, and pretend to like the food even if you don't. Korean cuisine isn't my favorite, and it's not Keanu's, either. Yet, I want him to know his heritage. Besides, you were the one who suggested ordering from the place."

"I did suggest it. Do you know why?"

"Enlighten me."

"I'm a considerate guy."

"Yes, you are," she says, indulging me with a sweet smile.

"Now that we've established my good guy cred, we need to do something about how fucking hot it is in this trailer."

"I'll turn on more fans."

"Or we can pack up the kid and the delivery food and head to my air-conditioned condo."

"Dayton, as much as I like that idea, I have to work tomorrow. Also, your condo has nowhere for Keanu to sleep. I know you don't like it here, but your place isn't set up for kids."

Her words give me an idea. First, I need to find a place to sit comfortably. Keanu jumps around the living room, making explosion noises from his plane shooting targets.

"Are you at war?" I ask him while Harmony turns on a fan and points it at me.

Keanu does his double-shoulder shrug and returns to shooting invisible enemies. I'm about ten degrees cooler by the time we hear a knock on the door. Harmony goes to answer, but I beat her to it.

"Could be a man. I better handle it."

After a little eye roll, she backs away and gestures for me to take charge. I answer the door and take the food from

102

the redneck on the other side. Giving him a dark frown, I make clear he isn't welcome here.

Once I shut the door, Harmony shakes her head. "So neighborly."

"He ain't your neighbor."

"Actually, Timmy lives in the Whisper Brooks Trailer Park down the road. He used to deliver for Pizza Hut. I didn't know he'd found a job delivering for the only Korean place in thirty miles. Good for him."

"I stopped following the gossip mills a long time ago. They never get any of the details right," I say, setting the food bag on the kitchen cart. "The gossips claim you seduced me. Shit, can't they give a guy his due?"

Harmony snickers at my expression while opening the takeout containers. "The nerve of some people."

I kiss the top of her head and look over the food. "What is it?" I ask since Harmony ordered using my phone.

"I ordered you japchae, which is Korean stir fry," she says and then opens another container. "This is bibimbap for Keanu."

"Why is there an egg in there? Gross."

"Don't be a baby," she says, tugging at my hair.

"What's this?"

"Galbitang is short rib soup. I think it's yummy. Now before you write off this new food, can I give you a little motherly advice? Try a little of everything, and then you can order your pizza."

"Yes, Mommy," I whisper in her ear. "Hey, maybe that'll be our next role-playing game."

"Now, you're being gross."

Harmony pushes me away, but I catch her grinning. She gets the food ready at the tiny kitchen table and calls Keanu to wash his hands. He's still jumping around and doesn't stop even while soaping up his fingers. Finally, I watch him settle in his chair and look over the food.

"Wow," he says to his toy man.

"Doesn't take much to impress him."

Harmony gives me a mama bear frown before joining Keanu at the table. I consider sitting with them, but there's no damn room. I look over the stir fry and decide I've eaten worse. More than once, I've left pizza out for over a day and still chowed down. Of course, I was usually drunk when I fearlessly ignored the wellbeing of my life and stomach.

"It's pretty good," I say, eating near the sink.

Keanu smiles with his mouth full. He's cute when he grins that way. The kid looks just the beautiful woman who's gotten me eating strange food and thinking about redecorating my condo.

To my surprise, Harmony inspires me to upend my entire life to make room for her and the kid she made with another man.

TWENTY-EIGHT — HARMONY

My mom's thick dark brown hair goes up in a bun as soon as spring arrives. It stays in the bun until late fall when the leaves change. I love how predictable she can be.

All my life, she's remained a rock, despite her changing jobs and occasional men. Her consistency is why I know I'll hear a speech soon about how Dayton means well, but I need to think about what kind of role model he is for Keanu.

She waits until Dayton's spent two nights at my place before ambushing me in the parking lot once I arrive home from work.

"You look so pretty," she says, fixing my shirt.

"So do you."

Mom smiles softly. "I see Dayton's Harley isn't here yet."

"No, it's not."

"Is he living with you now?"

"I would have mentioned if he was."

Mom caresses my arm where Millie dug her nails in yesterday.

"How is Keanu handling a man around?"

"He thinks Dayton is weird. He says the same thing about Billy and Camden. I think Bonn is the only man he doesn't feel is odd. Interesting, huh?"

I start walking toward Charlie's trailer, where Keanu waits. Mom follows along, silently plotting.

"Spill it," I say when we reach the trailer.

"I haven't quite figured out my angle. I'll wait to see how far this thing goes with Dayton."

"I appreciate your honesty, but I am aware Dayton is a wild card. I'm rolling with things now since I deserve an adventure in my life."

"I worry about Keanu."

"I survived your various boyfriends, and Ruby survived when you married Daisy's dorky dad. Kids are tough."

Mom narrows her gaze, realizing I'm too prepared for this discussion.

"You know what you're doing," she says, not believing her words for a minute.

"And I know if something goes wrong, I'll have you there to help me pick up the pieces."

Nodding, Mom gives me a sly grin. She underestimated how much I'd expected her meddling. Next time, she'll be better prepared.

I knock and wait for Charlie to unlatch the screen door. Keanu arrives first and yells my name. I lean down to where he smooshes his face against the screen.

"Did you miss me?"

Keanu shows Carl to me. "We ate macaroni and cheese."

Charlie appears behind Keanu and unlocks the door. "He had two bowls."

"I was hungry," Keanu says, diving into my arms.

While I carry my little man to our trailer, Mom remains with Charlie. I think I hear them talking about Dayton, but I might just be paranoid.

Once inside our place, Keanu takes off my shoes. He's really into laces lately and thinks my colorful tennis shoes are cool.

"Baby, is it okay if Dayton comes over later?" I ask once we're barefoot and chilling on the floor.

Keanu nods and shows me the puzzle he wants to play.

"Do you like Dayton?"

"He's big."

"He is big, but do you think he's nice?"

"He gave me pepperoni."

"Yep."

Keanu isn't interested in talking about Dayton. He's waited all day to tell me about his nap dream about poop. Plus, there are puzzles to play. He also needs to fix my hair by sticking plastic flowers in it. Yeah, my boy has plenty of plans for tonight. None of them involve worrying if my boyfriend might be a bad influence.

TWENTY-NINE — DAYTON

Funny how quickly a man can become obsessed. I used to think of Harmony a lot. Daily. Okay, probably hourly. But fantasizing about her sexiness was a comfortable feeling. I managed to go through my day with her constantly in my thoughts, yet never felt distracted.

Now, I'm restless whenever away from Harmony.

My problem isn't my dick. Dealing with a hard-on is something I'm used to after two years without sex. Fuck if I haven't become a ninja masturbator. I've nearly hit the point where I jack off just with my mind.

No, I miss knowing she's nearby. I try thinking about her at work, but I have no frame of reference about what her job's like. So, I imagine her back at her overheated trailer with the boy. Except she isn't there, and I can't join her.

I even get to thinking about Keanu. Is he napping? Eating child-sized food? Watching a bright movie with too much singing? I still hate how he reminds me of Ji-Hoon, but I dig how he reminds me of Harmony. He's her kid, and I'm warming up to how he's part of the package.

By the time I finish painting the walls with JJ at the refurbished building, I'm ready to get away from his annoying ass and spend time with my woman and her boy. That's a solid way to end a day. Now, I get why Camden chases Daisy around like a trained dog.

I arrive at the trailer, ready to convince Harmony to go out for dinner. She won't have to cook, and I can get a break from the hot box she calls home.

Her front door stands open, and I hear agitated voices. I pick up my speed, ready for a fight. I look inside to find Harmony on her knees, searching under the couch. Keanu is pulling toys out of his play box.

"Where is he?" Keanu asks, wide-eyed. "I lost him?"

Harmony searches behind the pillows on the couch, "Mama will look for Carl."

"What's Carl?" I ask, still ready to punch whoever caused their panic.

Harmony looks at me and then stands up. "His LEGO friend. You know, the little toy he carries with him everywhere. We can't find it."

"Doesn't he usually take it with him to daycare?"

"Yes, but Charlie couldn't find it this afternoon. So, we're looking here."

Keanu follows his mother around the trailer as she searches every corner, under every piece of furniture, and behind every toy. The longer they can't find it, the more freaked the kid gets. He finally stands in the middle of the living room and starts bawling.

"I lost Karl!" Keanu wails, tears running down his face.

Harmony picks up the boy and walks to the couch, where she holds him against her.

"Grandma is looking at her trailer, and Charlie is looking at hers. Billy is looking around the park. Even Aunt Ruby is looking at her condo, just in case."

"I lost my friend," Keanu sobs against her.

"I know it hurts, baby, but it'll be okay."

Unsure what to do with myself, I walk into the bedroom and look around. I remember the LEGO man was like two inches long with a sorta bald head and a red shirt. I only saw the top of him since Keanu always had the toy gripped in his tiny hand.

I find plenty of LEGOs scattered around the place, mostly under the bed. None are people. Returning to the living room, I find Keanu sliding off his mom's lap.

"Maybe he's in bed."

The boy runs to his room, leaving a clearly depressed Harmony.

"He loves that toy so much," she says, nearly in tears.

For whatever asshole reason, I turn into my fucking dad and say, "Well, then, maybe he should have taken better care of it."

Harmony's sad gaze shifts to anger in a blink of an eye. She looks at me like I'm scum on the bottom of her shoe.

"If you have no heart, what are you good for?" she hisses.

Despite the anger in her voice, tears fill her pale green eyes. She's brokenhearted over a piece of plastic. That's how much her kid matters to her. He's miserable, so she is, too.

This is how Harmony loves. It's how my mom was when I was growing up. Fuck, the woman still makes me pies and does my laundry. Good mamas love to their core, and that's how Harmony is with Keanu.

"What do you want me to say?" I ask when she stares with her wet, pissed eyes. "Do you want me to say it kills me to see you and the kid cry? Well, it does. But those are just words, and words don't fix shit."

"Not everything can be fixed, Dayton. Sometimes, it's just about surviving the pain and learning to live with it. Yeah, it's a toy, but it's his friend. He doesn't have many things he loves. First, Daisy leaves. Then, Ruby and Elle move away. In his life, a ten-minute drive might as well be a million miles away. Now, he's lost the friend he's talked to every day for a year. It's his favorite thing, and I can't fix his pain. I can only give him lots of love until he accepts Carl is gone."

"I can run to the store to get him a new one."

"He doesn't want a new toy. He wants his friend. You still don't get how you can't fix some things. Not with money or words. You can only give someone love while they adjust to their pain."

I realize she's talking about more than the toy. She lost her dad and Keanu's dad. She didn't love them, but she missed out because they're gone. Yet, she didn't stop moving forward. A poor chick like her can't stop living and working and existing because of heartache and loss. That's what Sally taught her kids. Life doesn't always work out, but you need to keep going.

My parents bought their way out of problems. They got new things to replace old things. My father didn't like marriage, so he banged random chicks. My mother lost her first husband, so she got a new one.

109

That's how my life has been until I messed up with Harmony. No matter what I did, I got a do-over. A second chance was always handed to me because I'm Dayton Rutgers, and my mom is a Hallstead. Everything can be fixed with enough money, violence, or power.

Now I'm a useless hump while my woman consoles her kid as he walks crying out of his room. I hate the way his face crumples up, and he whimpers in her arms. I can't stand the way Harmony fights against her mama bear tears. I want to run away and search for a fix, but I don't run and not only because there is no fix.

I don't run because there's nowhere else I belong.

THIRTY — HARMONY

Maybe I'm not cut out to be a mother and have a relationship. Other women handle it, but I completely shut down with Dayton while dealing with a heartbroken Keanu. My mama bear instincts make everything else fall away.

Dayton doesn't leave the trailer, even though he must be bored and frustrated with our evening. I hold Keanu, who alternates between watching his favorite movies and crying over his missing friend.

Every sound outside causes my baby to stare full of hope at the door. My mom and her friends are still searching for the little LEGO man. Every time he gets his hopes up, and then no one knocks on the door, Keanu looks to me for comfort.

I know he won't sleep without Carl, so I don't even attempt to put him to bed. Instead, he dozes off in my arms a little before ten. I carry him to his room and consider joining Dayton back in the living room.

Instead, I crawl into Keanu's bed, cover us with a blanket, and listen to him sleep. I know I'll start crying if I return to the living room.

My son needs me to be calm. Dayton does, too. If he says something stupid or cruel, I don't think I can keep from kicking his ass out the door.

So, I avoid starting a fight with a man still trying to figure out how to care about someone other than himself. I can't give him any of me tonight. My heart belongs to my sleeping son.

Around midnight, Keanu wakes up once and looks for Carl.

"I dream he came back," he mumbles.

"We'll look for him again tomorrow," I promise, caressing his soft skin and praying the toy shows up.

The rest of the night is quiet. I sleep well despite resting on a bed not suited for my length. Waking before Keanu, I walk into the kitchen and start the coffee. Seeing his boots at the front door, I know Dayton didn't take off. I peek in my room to find the handsome man spread out on my bed.

I leave him to sleep while I shower and get ready for work. Soon, I wake Keanu and dress him for daycare. He asks about Dayton, but I don't let him check on the naked man.

Charlie opens the door to her trailer and gives Keanu a big smile. Yet, I see something in her eyes. She leans down to look at him and then reveals Carl in her hand.

"You found him!" Keanu cries, taking his toy.

"The dog got hold of him. Got rough, too."

Keanu looks at his toy's face and finds it riddled with bite marks. Showing me, he seems ready to cry.

"Mama, you fix him?"

I run my fingers over the plastic and exhale sadly. "No, baby. I don't think I can."

Keanu rubs the messed-up part and begins sobbing. I don't know what to do. I need to go to work, but my baby craves his mama. Hell, maybe I'm not even capable of holding a job while being a good parent.

Charlie picks up Keanu and tells me to go to work. She promises he'll be fine soon and they'll call me in an hour. Despite her reassuring words, I'm in tears as I walk away. Keanu reaches for me, begging his mama to stay and make things better.

After bawling my eyes out on the way to the group home, I'm a red-faced mess when I arrive. The overnight staff member waits until I clean up and get my shit together. I'm in the middle of my early day routine when Charlie sends me a picture of a smiling Keanu holding Carl, just like old times.

Kids are resilient. More so than adults, considering I still feel like crap for the rest of the day. I nurse my sob-induced headache until three when my shift ends. Finally, I can head home to Keanu.

"We played, Mama," he says, showing me the battered Carl in his hand. "He's okay now."

Smiling, I pick him up and carry them both back to our trailer, where I expect to find Dayton. Though the trailer is empty, the fans remain on.

I make Keanu a snack before sitting down to text Dayton. He didn't message me all day. I avoided engaging with him while in a bad mood.

"Where are you?" I text twice before he responds.

"Sometimes, a man needs to get stone-cold drunk to make sense of his life."

"What does that mean?"

"Don't wait up."

I text him again, asking where he's at and if he's okay. I don't know why I'm worried. Dayton's a big boy. He's also a fan of the bottle, and I wouldn't blame him for needing a break from the drama at the trailer.

Despite the good reasons to let Dayton be Dayton, I can't help worrying he'll realize the meaning of his life doesn't involve Keanu and me.

THIRTY-ONE — DAYTON

I leave Harmony's trailer with the intention of getting a shower in a decent-sized bathroom, where I don't bang my elbows on everything. I'll pick up clean clothes and shave. Finally, I can stop by a ribs place and eat a big lunch.

That part goes according to plan, but I get to feeling weird when I'm eating. My mind returns to the crying from the night before. I was a useless fuck with both Keanu and Harmony. Shit, I could have fucking disappeared, and no one would have cared.

What kind of man is so worthless?

I still think buying the kid a new toy should fix the problem. That's not the right answer, though. I don't get why something so small should create such trauma in a family with bigger problems.

Harmony's job ought to be considered an issue. She gets hit, scratched, and even bitten by her clients. Yet, she shrugs off her injuries even while crying over a lost piece of plastic. To me, that's her number one problem to be fixed.

But my view isn't the only one that matters in a relationship.

That's why Camden puts up with Daisy's three cats. Or why Mom accepts Erik's weeklong hunting trips a few times a year. And no doubt compromise is why Bonn still lives in the condo when he clearly wants to move to a house.

Except I don't know how to be a selfless guy. I never shared growing up. I certainly didn't fucking share once I was a man. If Camden wanted something from me, he had to take it by force. Same went for me. That's how things work in my world. Now, I'm part of Harmony's life, and her rules are different.

I stop by Red Barn to get a drink and think about how simple my feelings once were for her. I'd been fooling myself for sure. Yet, so often, I'd sat in this place and imagined taking her home. In my mind, I figured getting her to take a chance with me was the difficult part. Once she got a taste, I assumed she wouldn't be able to say no to me again.

I drink a few beers before I lose my edginess. Yeah, things will be okay between Harmony and me. I'll figure shit out like I always do. When JJ showed up in Hickory Creek, I was the only one who thought to stay close to him and play the slow con. That's the kind of patience I need with Harmony and the kid.

I lose count of my beers by the time Camden walks into the bar. People look at him and then glance at me. Twins are cute when they're kids, but we're not little boys anymore.

"Hello, brother," he says, sliding into the booth.

"What do you want?"

"I want to talk."

"Now, you want to bond, huh? That ship sailed, shithead."

"It'll never be too late for us. We're bonded, fuck-wad."

I roll my eyes at his wording and gesture for him to continue. "What do you want to talk about?"

"Do you want to make small talk first and allow me to ease into my inquisition? Or should I jump to the interrogation?"

"I sincerely don't give a shit what you do. I only plan to half-listen, anyway."

"I came by your place a few times, but you're never there."

Rubbing my bloodshot eyes, I shrug. "I've been at Harmony's. A fact you already know because no one in Hickory Creek can mind their own fucking business."

"How do you like her kid?"

"Did someone send you here to ask me that?"

"No, why would they?" Camden asks, wearing a sincere expression on his irresistible face.

"Then, why ask?"

"I'm going with the small talk before I get to my point."

"I don't have all night to listen to you ask questions I don't want to answer. Just get to your point and then get out."

"It's a public place, asshole."

115

"You never drink here."

"True. It's a loser bar for loser people."

People around us frown at him, but Camden just smiles at them. I don't, though. I glare hard at the looky-loos.

"Are you listening to club business?" I holler at them. "Get the fuck away from this booth!"

The anger in my voice sends the customers scurrying. Some of them leave the bar altogether, but most boozers just find a spot farther away.

"Well, that was one way to handle the situation," Camden says when I stop giving my death stare to everyone.

Using my arms as a pillow, I wish he would leave. "What do you want?"

"You've been hanging around JJ more than usual."

"Yeah, because he's jumping through hoops to get his patch. I'm the guy who has to hold his hand while he jumps."

"Well, you are his best friend."

I hear resentment in Camden's voice. *He's such a jealous little bitch.*

"Don't cry," I say with my face still hidden under my hair.

"Is JJ ready to quit?"

"Over some shit jobs? No," I reply, peeking out from behind my hair long enough to add, "Did you really think he would?"

"He seems like a lazy fuck."

I rub my eyes and sit up straight. "He might be, but he knows the shit he puts up with now will lead to a payday later."

"What does he talk about with you?" Camden asks and crosses his arms tightly.

"His old life. What women he wants to fuck. Mostly, he talks about Howler."

"What about him?"

"He wants to know what Howler was like when I was growing up? What Howler likes to eat? What movies does he prefers? What women has he fucked? JJ has a million questions about his father."

116

"Why not ask Howler?"

"The old man spends more time bragging about his long-lost son than spending time with him. You'd know that if you didn't spend all your time pitching a fit about JJ."

"I can't stand the fucker."

"No one can. However, he's here, and he has goals. You act as if he's got the plague won't let you close to him."

"Are you saying you're faking like you're his buddy?"

"Sure, why not? I fake the same shit with you all the time."

Camden smirks. "Asshole."

"If you need to cry, take it home to your woman and leave me alone."

"What about your woman?"

Thinking about Harmony makes me crave another beer. "I don't want to talk about my shit with you."

"And why is that?"

"You can't see past your dick."

"And you can?"

"I'm not our club's future president."

"Look, if you want to hash shit out, then let's do it."

I turn toward him and sigh loudly. "This is just like you. I'm here, minding my own fucking business. Then, you show up when I'm drunk half off my ass to cause trouble. Why can't you come at me when I'm sober and ready to fight?"

"I don't want to fight, but I expect you to be square with me for fucking once."

"And you pick now to make your big stand? Now, when I'm clearly feeling like shit is when you go for the jugular?"

Camden stands up, looking ready to storm out. I hope he does before I'm forced to punch his good-looking mug. My brother instead stares at me while I order another beer.

"You drink too much," he says, sitting back down.

"I know."

"Then why don't you drink less?"

"I have my reasons."

"Plan to share?"

"No."

Camden orders himself a second beer. "We used to be close."

"That was a long time ago."

"What happened?"

"Our world got bigger, and we had space to spread out. It didn't help that people always thought of us as the same person."

"That they do."

"We're not the same. You've been focused on running the club for as long as I can remember. As for me, I don't give a crap about leading. I'm fine as a foot soldier."

"Bullshit," Camden grumbles.

"No, it's not. I don't have the fire to call the shots like you do."

"That's the booze talking."

"Have it your way. I know what I know."

"I don't believe you've changed that much."

"Think what you want."

"I hope you don't think JJ can be VP. No way will I ever trust that fucker."

"Do what you want, boss. You're running the show."

"You know that ain't true."

Smiling at the pissy tone in his voice, I point out, "You got Dad running to you for help with JJ. He and Howler look like fools after Hayes and Bonn took over Common Bend. They're on their way out. You're the guy everyone expects to slide into the leadership role with the ease of a small dick in a stretched-out whore."

"Poetic."

"I don't know what you want."

"I want to know if you're keeping an eye on JJ."

"Is that my job now?"

"I assumed that's what you've been doing the last few months."

"No, you thought I was his best friend, and you got jealous. I remember laughing at you about that."

Camden frowns when I laugh at him now.

"I shouldn't talk to you when you're drunk."

"Yet, here you are, doing just that."

Camden throws cash on the table and stands up. "Fine. We'll talk again when you're sober. You know, assuming you ever go long enough without booze."

"If that's a hint that you're setting up an intervention, have at it. Just make sure to provide snacks. A man needs to eat."

Camden glances around the bar and then back at me. I know he's waiting for me to say something. *Should I tell him that I love him and he's my favorite brother? Would a hug help his sour mood? Maybe I can beg him not to leave because he's so special to me.*

Just thinking of those options makes me laugh while I rest my head on the table. I'm still snickering long after Camden stomps out of the bar and finally leaves me the fuck alone.

An hour later, I ask myself one simple question. How many times will I look at the bottom of an empty bottle before I know the answers aren't waiting for me there? I spend nearly a day drinking more booze than a man should tolerate. My problems don't go away, of course. I'm not who I need to be for Harmony while she's everything I crave.

I walk my Harley most of the way to Lush Gardens. Driving would have been faster, but I nearly hit a parked car and then a tree. Even walking, I don't see where I'm going and get pretty close to losing a nut when I collide with a fire hydrant.

Dragging my ass to Harmony's front door, I don't know what time it is. The moon is bright in the sky, meaning I've been drinking for most of the day.

The beers make me brave. No, more than that. They make me cocky and entitled. I want Harmony. She's mine. Anyone, including her, who doesn't agree is a problem to be finessed. I'll fix whatever needs fixing because I'm Dayton Rutgers, and I get what I fucking want.

I knock twice before Harmony's beautiful face appears at the curtain. She studies me, and I catch her letting out a defeated sigh. Despite her annoyed expression, she opens the door.

"It's late, Dayton," she says through the crack.

119

Pushing on the door, I announce, "I am not a piece of garbage."

"Are you drunk?" she asks, already knowing the answer since I stink of booze.

"I don't need liquor to tell me I deserve what I want, and I want you."

Glancing back at Keanu, Harmony looks horrified. When her gaze meets mine, I try to kiss her.

"You need to go," she mumbles against my lips.

"Why? Do you have a man in here?"

"Are you frigging dense, Rutgers? I'm watching 'The LEGO Movie' with my son. Be smart and get your crap together."

"I am smart," I say, pushing my way past her into the trailer. "I know what I want. Why shouldn't I get it?"

Rather than shut the door, Harmony instead stares disgusted at me. I reach around her and pull it closed.

"I'm staying."

"I know your mother raised you with better manners."

"Oh, you know that, do you? What else do you know?" I demand, glaring down at her. "Do you know how I can't stop thinking about you? Do you know how you break my fucking heart every time you blow me off?"

As Harmony's angry eyes mellow, she sighs. "This isn't the time."

"It's never the time."

Shifting back and forth on her heels, Harmony doesn't answer me. She looks at Keanu, who is nervous about my presence. He thinks I'm a madman, and I don't blame him.

As much as I scare him, Keanu wants to watch his movie. He finally peels his gaze away from his mom long enough to stare at the TV.

"He should be mine," I tell Harmony. "You know that."

"Well, he's not. We never happened, and you can't change the past."

"What about the future?" I say, cupping her face. "He doesn't have a dad, and I can be one to him."

"You once said kids were a burden to a man like you."

"I say a lot of shit."

120

"That's the problem, Dayton. You say lots of shit. Why should I believe any of it?"

"Because you know he should be mine because you should have been mine. It's not too late. We're not dead. We should embrace the risky choice."

Harmony's resolve begins to crack. "I'm afraid to take the leap and have you not there on the other side."

"You think I'm a piece of shit."

My voice is too loud, and I draw Keanu's gaze back to us. A pissed Harmony sighs. She'll try to make me leave soon, but I won't go. Fighting with her doesn't fix the pain in my chest, but I can't walk away again. *I know how that always turns out.*

I press her hand against my chest. "I'm dying without you. No amount of booze makes me forget."

Harmony takes pity on me. Not only do I see forgiveness in her gaze, but she also doesn't immediately remove her hand.

"You can stay for a while, but no yelling."

When I walk to the couch, I stare down at Keanu. His father didn't want him or Harmony. If I got her pregnant, I would have married her and raised the boy. Instead, Keanu belongs to a dead man.

"The past is crap," I say, sitting on the floor. "Your mother is a god."

"Stop acting weird," Harmony says, pulling me back so I rest against the couch.

Sitting with her legs crossed behind me, Harmony leans my head back. She caresses the side of my face from temple to jaw.

"Calm yourself," she whispers.

Keanu watches his mother until she smiles at him. "Dayton had a bad day. He's hot now and needs to relax."

He jumps up and runs into another room. When he returns, Keanu carries a paddle fan. He begins waving it next to my face to cool me off.

"Breathe deeply," Harmony whispers as her fingers wash away the top layer of my tension.

The millions of other layers remain long after Keanu is distracted by "The LEGO Movie." The boy sits a foot from the TV and talks along with the dialogue.

I twist around to look at Harmony. "Life handed me everything, and I shit it the fuck away."

"What are you complaining about now?" she asks in her silky soft voice.

"You have a kid and work with disabled people. You're used to dealing with people who can't communicate right. How can you not understand me?"

"Maybe I don't want to understand what you're saying."

"Why?"

"I have a mind of my own, Dayton Rutgers. Isn't it possible my vision for the future doesn't include your demands?"

"It should."

"Why?"

"I can give you things."

"I don't want things."

"I can make you happy."

"You can't even make yourself happy."

Closing my eyes, I search for the right words. "I'd walk away from the club for you. I'd leave behind everything to be with you."

Harmony covers my mouth with her hand. "Don't say such things. The club is your family."

"You should be my family."

"Why?" she asks, giving me a confused frown.

"You know why."

"I think you see me as a panacea."

Frowning, I ask, "A what?"

"A fix to your problems. You're unhappy, and you think I have the power to make everything better. But I'm not a magic bullet to kill your demons. I'm a woman with her own problems."

Leaning closer, I inhale her baby powder scent. I also smell a hint of what I think is raspberry. I ache to taste her skin. Harmony senses where my thoughts are headed because she shakes her head as a warning.

"I wasn't broken until you," I tell her, unsure if what I'm saying is even true.

"You're not broken. You're obsessed."

"I can't pretend anymore. I thought I was a strong fucker by not crawling after you. But really, I was a weak piece of shit unable to admit what I need. Now, I'm laying it all out."

"So, I must instantly give in to you?"

"You need me, too."

"I desire you. That's true. I don't know if I'd call that need."

"We're more than the fucking."

Harmony covers my mouth and shakes her head. "You claim you want me, but I come with a child that doesn't need your dirty mouth spouting cuss words like they're punctuation."

I glance back at Keanu entranced by his movie. "How many times has he seen this?"

"A million, probably."

"Is that healthy?"

When Harmony yanks on my hair, I witness the full wrath in her faded green eyes.

"Stop being..." Harmony's so angry that she can't speak. "This. If you want to stay, you better earn my attention."

"I'm losing my mind," I whisper. "I don't know how many times a kid should watch a movie. I don't know how anything works anymore."

"Maybe you need medical help."

"I need you."

"What if I'm not enough?"

"You were where I went wrong. I had you in the palm of my hand. I only needed to close the deal, and I pussied out. I know things would be different if I made my move back then. I've known that for years. Now, I am drowning in those fucking regrets."

"You feel it now because Camden has a wife. You want what he has."

Sighing, I wonder if she's right. "I thought I was like my dad, and having a family was a mistake. I was wrong, and I gave you up."

"You keep talking like we would have worked out. There's no telling."

"My heart knows."

"Doesn't my heart matter, too?"

"Yes, and you also feel it. It's why you haven't thrown me out. You know I can be the man you need."

"Stop talking until Keanu goes to bed. If you can't do that, you're not the man I deserve. Do you understand? Show me you're capable of caring about something beyond your needs."

Harmony's tone sobers me up a little. However, I still want to crawl on top of her and fuck away my bad mood.

Instead, I keep my ass planted on the floor and stare at the TV, where LEGOs sing about individualism or maybe conformity. I'm too drunk to figure out the song's point. Either way, Keanu bobs his little head to the music, and his movements lull me into a boozy dream.

THIRTY-TWO — HARMONY

What have I gotten myself into with Dayton? Things were so simple back when we drank and made out in the safety of the Red Barn Bar. Now, he's passed out on the floor of my house, only a foot from where my innocent boy alternates between watching the movie and fanning the snoring hunk.

I sit on the couch, studying the two guys in my life. They are so completely different, yet they both have me wrapped around their fingers.

No way would any other man survive doing what Dayton just pulled. I'd have called Mom and told her to bring her gun if anyone crashed on my floor like this. But for Dayton, I pretend he's sick.

"I get sick?" Keanu asks while I tuck him in bed.

"Nope. It's not that type of sick. Dayton ate something bad and took too much medicine. Do you remember how Aunt Daisy took too much medicine and walked into the wall that time?"

Keanu nods. "She fell down."

"Yeah, but she was okay the next day. Dayton will be, too."

"He was hot, and I had my fan."

"You're a good helper."

A smiling Keanu checks to see if Carl is properly tucked in bed.

"Is it okay if Dayton sleeps here tonight? He's scared of being alone when he's sick."

"He snored."

"Yep."

"Mama, do I snore?"

"Sometimes," I say, tickling his tummy. "Like when you have a cold or get allergies."

125

Keanu likes the idea of snoring. Resting on his side, he pretends Carl is snoring now. I sit on the edge of the bed until his eyes get heavy.

Kissing his head, I leave him and the no longer snoring toy. In the living room, I find Dayton isn't snoring, either.

"You ditched me," he says, sitting on the floor.

The sight of his long legs stretched out in my small trailer makes me think of a giant in Lilliput. Dayton doesn't fit in this room any better than he fits in my life. Yet, I can't ask him to leave either of them.

Walking to where he leans partly against the wall and half on the couch, I say, "Take off your shoes."

Dayton only stares at me with his bleary eyes, so I lean down and yank off his boots. Walking to the front door, I drop them next to mine and Keanu's. They dwarf our shoes, making me think of the difference between my two men. One is a temperamental child in need of constant attention. The other is my three-year-old son.

Returning to where Dayton remains slumped, I sigh and wonder if I should leave him where he's at and head to bed.

"Now, wait here," he babbles, reaching for my long skirt and tugging me closer. His hand disappears up the fabric and caresses my inner thighs. "You want rid of me."

"Dayton, just sleep off this crap, and we'll talk in the morning."

"I don't want to talk. Words smell up my brain."

I start to laugh at his babble. However, the giggles get stuck in my throat once his fingers tug down my panties.

"Dayton, don't," I whisper, torn between letting him rest and the urge to spread my legs a bit more so he can slide his fingers inside me. "Keanu's in the next room."

"He doesn't know to get up," Dayton says, or at least, I think that's what his gibberish means.

Lifting my skirt, his head disappears under the cloth. I stare at the short hallway leading to Keanu's room. I don't want my baby scarred for life. Then again, he'd have no idea what Dayton was doing to me. Though, he might be terrified by the moans I'm hiding behind my hand.

Dayton tugs down my panties and slides them off one foot and then the other. With nothing keeping his lips from my flesh, I lean against the wall just behind me and lift one of my legs.

Dayton doesn't waste time teasing. His tongue dives deep between my damp flesh and licks feverishly. Before I can adjust to the feel of him inside me, his lips discover my clit. Dayton latches on like a man on a mission. Sucking hard, he grips my thighs and forces my legs wider.

I moan behind my hand while fucking his mouth. I'm close to an orgasm instantly, but I can't let go. Not when my gaze remains locked on the hallway, where my baby might appear at any time.

Dayton won't be denied my orgasm. His lips increase their painfully wonderful pressure while he finger-fucks me. I cover my mouth with a second hand and cry out behind them. The pleasure blinds me. My eyes shut as I struggle against the kind of sensations no vibrator will ever provide.

I never regain my composure before Dayton appears from my skirt. He stands in an easy motion, even while his fingers pump inside me.

With his other hand, he undoes his jeans and shoves them and his boxers down. His fingers finally relent long enough for him to grab my hips and lift me up. Mere seconds pass before his fingers are replaced by his cock.

"Oh," I grunt, and my pussy immediately sucks hungrily at his flesh. "The bedroom, Dayton."

He doesn't hear me or understand while he thrusts into my body, harder and faster.

"Bedroom," I say again while he yanks up my shirt and exposes my bra. "Dayton, it's like three feet away. Go."

Without saying a word, he shuffles toward my bedroom. His pants come off halfway there, and he kicks them aside before stepping into my dark room. Shoving me against the wall, he yanks up my bra and spits on my right nipple. His fingers work at my hard flesh with the same painful frenzy as his hips pump into my body.

No longer worried about Keanu seeing, I grip Dayton's shoulders and work with his rough rhythm. Fucking against a wall is a new thing for me. Yet, I manage to wrap my arms around his neck and bounce wildly on his cock.

"I want to bite your nipples," he growls in my ear while his hips move faster. "I want to come in your mouth."

Dayton slaps my ass, startling me. My pussy reacts by tightening around him and refusing to let go. Dayton leans his head back and smiles. His balls release the heat of his seed into my clenching pussy.

"Best fuck of my life," he says and turns toward my bed.

Dumping me on the mattress, Dayton grabs my skirt and tugs it off.

"Show me your pussy," he demands, turning on the light.

"Close the bedroom door."

"Open your legs."

Even thoroughly appreciative after being well fucked, I slam my legs together. "Shut the bedroom door, Dayton Rutgers."

Rolling his eyes, he reaches over and closes the bedroom door. When his gaze returns to me, he gestures at my legs.

"Open them and show me."

Relenting, I reveal my glistening pussy. Dayton smiles at the sight of it and then crawls on the bed so he can remove my bra.

"I'm going to bite your tits." Dayton lowers his mouth and nips my left nipple. "Did that asshole see your nipples?"

"No," I say, closing my eyes while he sucks and bites at the excited flesh. "He fucked me in the back seat of a car with us mostly dressed. You're the only man who's tasted them."

Dayton glares at me. "I'm going to fuck you so hard."

"Because you like my tits?"

"They're mine. I'm going to fuck them, too. I'm going to fuck every inch of you. Nothing will stop me. Not even you."

Dayton is so full of shit, as usual. Even drunk, his teeth entice my nipples more than punish them. Though I'm

128

fucked hard enough to nearly crack open my skull on the headboard. Of course, not shoving a pillow between my head and a hard object was an amateur move on my part.

The best moment of our night together isn't the intense orgasms but holding Dayton against me after he passes out for the second time. His last words before crashing make my heart feel better than any part of my body.

"Loving you scares the shit out of me," he whispers after coming inside me for the last time. His body rests on mine, and his face snuggles my hair. "But I came back, and I always will."

THIRTY-THREE — DAYTON

Since the kid quickly recovered from his freak out over losing his toy, the least I can do is bounce back from my freak out over his meltdown.

Sober again, I get started on the plans for my condo. I've never believed in waiting, but I did for Harmony. I've also never wanted to change, but here I am again taking the leap for my woman.

JJ walks in through the condo's open front door. I stand near the balcony, watching men paint the place. Tomorrow, the carpet will be installed, followed by the new furniture. As much as I hate getting up this early, someone needs to keep an eye on the progress.

"What's all this?" JJ asks, joining me.

"I'm redecorating to make it more lady-and-kid friendly."

JJ peeks into the second bedroom, where the once empty space receives a fresh coat of light blue paint.

"I hired a decorating broad to help me fix up the place," I explain while walking into the second bedroom. "She bought a light for this room that'll make the ceiling look like ocean waves. Harmony's kid likes fish and got dreamy-eyed at the zoo's aquarium. I figure he'll dig it in here and stay in his bed rather than jumping in mine."

"Are they moving in?" JJ asks, looking as if he smells a fart.

"No, but I want to be able to bring her over for the weekend. She won't leave the kid for that long. This way, I gain access to her without having to hang out at the trailer park. Makes me edgy to spend time around people I sell product to."

"I get that you want easier access to your chick's pussy, but this still seems like a lot of shit for a kid that ain't yours," JJ says, looking around the room.

I walk out of the second bedroom and away from the paint fumes. JJ follows me, stepping over the supplies on the ground. We end up on the balcony, where I lift my face to the sun.

"Harmony comes with a kid, and I want her," I say with my face still upward.

"In the animal kingdom, when a new alpha male takes over a lion's pride, it'll kill the offspring of the last alpha."

"Are you suggesting I murder a three-year-old?" I ask, cocking an eyebrow.

"Naw, I'm just saying it ain't natural to look after the offspring of another man."

"Did your mommy's boyfriends tell you that?" When JJ shoots me a dirty look, I smile. "You're too sensitive."

"I'm just saying you can't even pretend he's yours. Not when he's got those slanty eyes and—"

My elbow pops JJ in the nose before my brain catches up with what I'm doing. After a second of internal surprise, I chuckle and pat his back.

"Sorry, man."

"What the fuck?" he grumbles, cupping his bloody nose.

"I know you don't understand loyalty, but you need to catch a hint. People defend what's theirs. Harmony is mine, and her kid is part of a package deal."

JJ doesn't even try to get my point, so I shift to a topic he'll understand.

"It's like the club. If you want to be a member, you can't only think of yourself. You can't fuck with people connected to the members. You gotta know how to put the group before your needs. That's something you didn't get growing up. But you'll learn now with the club. Disloyal fuckers don't get patches."

"You could've told me that without busting my nose."

"Trust me. This way is better. You'll remember what I'm teaching if it comes with a little pain."

"Teach me what?"

"Don't talk shit about my woman and her kid. That's personal, and a man reacts to personal shit by lashing out.

131

You'd know that if you viewed anyone as yours instead of an obstacle standing in your way."

"That's bullshit," he mutters, still wiping blood from his nose.

"I see the way you get whenever you think I might not be putting you first. That won't work in a club where loyalty is king. You've got to be willing to die for those guys. Or take a longer sentence to protect your people. That's loyalty, not making yourself look good first and worrying about everyone else later."

JJ frowns at me and walks to the kitchen, where he washes off his bloodied face. I follow him and lean against the counter, waiting for him to finish up.

"What will you do if it comes down to protecting the club or leaving your woman and her kid alone so you can do time?"

"Depends," I say, giving him one of those double shoulder shrugs Keanu does. "If my club takes care of my family, I'll do the long stretch to protect them. But that's not even a question with the Brotherhood."

JJ balls up a handful of paper towels and presses them against his nose. "I didn't mean any harm. The kid ain't yours, and I don't want a woman pulling a fast one on you. I saw enough of that shit with my mom and the games she played with me."

As much as I'd like to punch JJ again, I only smile. "I appreciate you watching out for me. That's the kind of loyalty the club rewards."

JJ mimics my smile, but he's pissed. Before arriving in Hickory Creek, he was an asshole who smacked anyone that looked at him wrong. Now, he's forced to eat shit from people he'd rather put down with a bullet.

His smile fades when he hears Camden's voice in the hallway. My brother enters the condo and looks around. Bonn appears a few seconds later.

"Where's all your shit?" Camden asks, walking to where the couch normally rests.

"Got rid of it. I'm getting new stuff."

"It's weird being in here without the dark walls," Bonn says.

Before today, my condo was painted a midnight blue. I kept the place as dark as possible to make sleep easier in the day. The designer suggested a silver-blue would be soothing to children and appeal to someone with Harmony's pastel-favored tastes.

"You fuckers are jealous you didn't think to fix up your condos back when you were romancing your ladies."

Camden smiles until he notices JJ. I swear my brother can't fake a single thing when it comes to his handsome fucking face. I bet my sister-in-law is happy to know the man lies like shit.

"What happened to your nose?"

JJ glares hard at Camden. "Dayton elbowed me."

"How come?"

"Lover's spat," I tell Camden, who frowns darker.

Even smiling at how I've pissed off both men, I wish I didn't love fucking with people so much. My life would likely be a whole lot simpler. *Yet, no doubt duller, too.*

THIRTY-FOUR — HARMONY

Dayton puts on a casual smile, but I know he's up to something. I'm seriously worried about what it might be.

Opening the door to his condo, he waves me inside. I hold Keanu's hand and shuffle past Dayton.

The few glimpses I've gotten of his condo over the years made me wonder if he was into the occult. Everything was dark and gloomy. Dayton never impressed me as emo, but who knew what he was like behind closed doors.

Now, the walls are a lovely silvery blue. The once-covered windows reveal the condo's view. Beneath my feet, I notice he's carpeted the entire entrance and family room.

This is not the condo of Dayton Rutgers. No, it's where a stylish woman might live when she wasn't spending weekends doing something trendy.

"Why did you change stuff?" I ask like a moron.

Dayton shuts the door and joins me where the galley kitchen's island overlooks the living room.

"It was suited for a bachelor, but I'm a taken man now."

"Oh, really?" I ask, tugging at his shirt with my free hand.

"I wanted to make it more appealing to you, so you'd sleep over."

"That's sweet of you."

Dayton squats down next to Keanu. "Bud, I made up the extra room for you. That way, you can stay close to your mama."

Keanu doesn't understand ninety percent of what Dayton just said, but he smiles anyway.

Standing up, Dayton wears a proud smile, and I know he's up to something. He takes my hand and tugs me toward the second bedroom.

I figured Dayton decked out the room with a bed and a few toys. No way did I consider what he put together.

"Wow," I say, wide-eyed as we enter the sea-themed room.

The treasure chest-style double bed is covered with a blanket with different anchor designs. The walls are ocean blue except for the one covered in LEGO boards. My eyes try to take in all the details, but I'm overwhelmed.

"Wow," I mumble again.

"Glad you like it," Dayton says and then leans down and looks at Keanu. "How about you? Think you could have fun in here?"

My baby is more freaked out than I am. He doesn't know what to look at first, but I catch him eyeing a bucket of LEGOs next to the board-covered wall.

"Can he play?" I ask, sounding overwhelmed.

"Sure, that's why it's here."

Keanu looks around and then at me, but he doesn't play.

"Isn't this room beautiful?" I ask him.

Nodding, Keanu whispers, "Wow."

I nearly burst into tears at the sight of his little face so filled with excitement. Barely holding myself together, I walk with him and sit on the floor next to the boards.

"Let's build something," I tell him.

Keanu looks in the bucket, still nervous to touch the shiny new toys. I glance back at Dayton and try to convey how much this means to Keanu and me. People rarely put us first, but he changed everything in his home for us.

I mouth the words, "Thank you."

Dayton smiles like the cockiest fucker in the world. If I didn't know he was a stone-cold killer, I'd think he was the sweetest man in the world and perfectly suited to fatherhood. The reality is far from that fantasy. Yet, right now, I'll let myself dream.

Keanu builds a house on the wall and giggles when I pretend like my person falls off.

"He can't walk," I say while he shows me how to hold him.

"Like this, Mama."

"Oh, I get it. Hey, can Dayton play with us?"

Keanu looks back at Dayton and pats the floor. I doubt the sexy man is interested in playing LEGOs, but he goes along with the game. Sitting on the ground, he takes a few pieces and snaps them together to make a Harley.

We play on the floor of this magical room for nearly an hour, creating a village for Carl and the new LEGO figures. Dayton names his guy "Champ" and has it ride his lame motorcycle creation.

While on the floor with my favorite two fellas, I forget about Dayton's baggage. I only know he's made my baby smile bigger than I've seen in a long time.

"I'll order pizza," Dayton says, reaching for his phone. "Can you stay tonight?"

Even without having overnight supplies, there's no way I can refuse Dayton. Not after what he did for us, and he's smiling like a kid himself.

Once the food arrives, Dayton gets things set up in the kitchen.

"Is it okay if we stay here tonight?" I ask Keanu when we're alone.

Looking around the room, Keanu is nervous about sleeping in a strange place. Yet, I also know he isn't ready to leave.

"Yes or no?" I ask when he says nothing.

"Yes, but you stay with me."

"I will, baby," I say, standing and holding out my hand. "We can't eat in here. The carpet is new and clean. Let's go to the kitchen."

Keanu picks up Carl and takes my hand. We find Dayton splitting the pizza and filling three plates.

"He won't eat that much," I say when Dayton gives Keanu two slices. "But it looks great."

Dayton's smile falters. Even in his thirties, he still needs his ego indulged. I guess I don't blame him. This family man's routine is new, and he's insecure. That was clear from his drunken binge last week.

To soothe his anxieties, I ask him for details about what he did to the condo. Dayton talks about the designer he hired and how he oversaw the work. Rather than find his bragging too much, I'm stunned by how sexy he is when he explains mundane things like carpet and paint samples.

Keanu whispers to Carl throughout dinner about Dayton and sleeping in the big bed. I'm torn between wanting to cuddle with my sweet baby and riding my sexy man.

Once Dayton turns on the ocean night light projector in the second bedroom, Keanu is overwhelmed. He nearly climbs me and wants to be held.

"Wow," he whispers.

"I know. Pretty cool, huh?"

Dayton watches nearby with an expression somewhere between pride and horniness. He no doubt hopes Keanu will crash soon, and he can receive his reward for a job well done.

"Ready for bed?" I ask after we've borrowed toothbrushes from Ruby down the hall.

Nodding excitedly, Keanu crawls up the little ladder into the big bed and wiggles himself under the covers. Before he speaks, I know he's afraid and wants me to stay with him. The room is beautiful, but it's also new and scary. When he stays at Ruby's, Keanu has Elle with him. *Sleeping alone isn't an option.*

I rest on top of the blankets and stare at his face. His wide eyes take in the sight of the lights on the ceiling.

"Water," he whispers to me.

"It does look like water. Just like fish swim in. Are you a fish?" I tease, giving his tummy a tickle.

Keanu laughs and wiggles away from my fingers. Though happy, he's tenser than I've seen him in a long time. Until very recently, his life remained consistent. Now, he's dealing with one change after another. I know he doesn't understand why he has a room at Dayton's place. Everything is too big and confusing for him.

Keanu's eyelids only get heavy when I hum his favorite song from "The LEGO Movie." He smiles while holding my fingers and watching the lights. I fall silent after ten minutes and wait for him to crash. Yet, every time I move, he whimpers my name.

"Mama's here," I promise, and he settles down.

"It's like the ocean," he says long after I expect him to sleep. "But it's not the ocean."

"No, it's just lights. You don't need to be scared."

Keanu nods but remains on edge. We rest like that for over an hour. Him on his back, staring at the ceiling while gripping my fingers. Me curled up on my side, watching his beautiful face. Between the quiet room and the relaxing lighting, I don't know which one of us falls asleep first.

THIRTY-FIVE — DAYTON

In my many fantasies about Harmony spending the night at my place, I never once considered I'd sleep alone. *How the hell is the kid getting more action than me?*

I sit in the living room, waiting for Harmony to appear from the second bedroom and reward me for my good deeds.

An hour later, I'm still waiting. A crappy Syfy movie isn't enough to keep me entertained. With my footsteps silent on the carpeted floor, I walk to the bedroom and peer inside.

With the blue lights swirling on the ceiling, I easily see Harmony's body curled up over the covers. Keanu is hidden on the other side of her, and I listen for any sign they're awake.

Stepping closer, I find Keanu face up with his eyes closed. In one hand, he holds his little toy. His other hand grips his mom's fingers. Even irritated to know my woman is sound asleep while my dick remains unloved, I can't deny they're a sweet sight. These are the two people I want to build a family with.

Leaving them to sleep, I return to the living room and hope Harmony wakes up before I also crash. This getting up early crap really wears out a man.

By midnight, I'm sulking when I walk to bed alone. This night was supposed to end with Harmony and me marking my new bed. Instead, I rest on my back and stare at the ceiling. When that doesn't work, I turn on the TV and think about rubbing one out just so I can get through the night.

"Are you sulking?" I hear from the door.

Harmony steps out of the darkness and into the light of the TV. The sight of her bed head makes my dick hard. A sleepy Harmony is a sexy-as-fuck Harmony.

"No," I mutter. "I enjoy loneliness."

"I will never forget what you did for Keanu," she says, climbing on the bed and removing her shirt. "You gave him more than I ever imagined for my baby."

I cup her tits and soak in the warmth of her body. Harmony covers my hands with hers while she straddles me.

"You're capable of such sweetness, Dayton Rutgers."

Plucking her nipple, I want to enjoy her compliments. Instead, my dick is running the show, and it's very aware of the heat coming from between her legs.

"You want to fuck," I growl before covering her lips with mine.

Harmony moans into my mouth. Pushing me back on the bed, she caresses my cock through my boxers. I lift my hips, searching for her pussy still hidden behind thin panties.

"Stop playing," I grunt, rolling her over so I can yank aside her underwear and slide my fingers into her damp pussy. "You want this."

Harmony doesn't answer with words. Instead, she tightens her muscles around my fingers, pressing harder against the knuckle teasing her clit.

My boxers are long past their expiration date, and I tear them off with one rough tug. I yank her panties free and toss them somewhere.

Lifting her leg with one hand, I guide the head of my cock to her waiting pussy. Harmony lifts her hips at the same moment I press mine down. We grunt in unison as I enter her in a rough thrust.

"I changed for you," I say through gritted teeth while my hips pump harder. "You owe me."

"Nope," she says, wrapping her legs around my waist and lifting her hips to meet my rhythm. "I owe no one nothing."

Her stubborn grin makes me want to come, but I need her pussy to suffer a little first. It's been waiting to be claimed since she walked into the condo. I want Harmony to feel me inside her long after leaving this bedroom. *Hell, I don't want her sitting comfortably for days.*

In fact, I want the entire world to know she's been properly fucked. I wonder if I can convince her to wear a hat saying just that.

Harmony reaches up and tugs at my hair when she comes. Her fingers twist tighter with my locks until the pain sends my balls over the edge.

"Bitch," I grumble, and she laughs.

Harmony is still grinning when I've fucked every drop into her hungry pussy.

She pushes me off her enough to roll out from under my body. "You remind me of pissy Missy Bumruck from the trailer park. She gets so mad when things don't go just her way. Are you a grumpy old woman, Dayton?"

"I have never enjoyed sex talk. Especially the shitty teasing kind."

"Poor rich boy," she says, smacking my ass.

Though I roll over to grab her, Harmony is faster than her sleepy eyes indicate. She straddles me again, pushing my shoulders against the mattress.

"You might be whiny," she whispers and gives my left nipple a tug with her teeth. "But you deserve a reward for making my baby so happy. Hmm, should you get more pussy, or do you need alone time with my tongue?"

"Why can't I have both?"

"Spoken like a true spoiled brat," she taunts before sliding down until her lips kiss my already thickening cock. "I always had a thing for big dicks. As a preteen, I saw a porno where the guy was hung."

For whatever fucking insane reason, I'm jealous thinking of her fantasizing about a movie slut. Harmony lathers my balls with her tongue before smiling up at me.

"He wasn't much to look at, but his cock was beautiful. Then, when I was a little older, I saw two people fucking in a parking lot. I watched him pull out of the chick so he could enjoy another hole. I felt naughty watching, but the entire thing was depressing. Want to know why?"

"Because you realized you're a perv?" I ask while she slides the head of my cock deep into her throat and gives it a few intense sucks.

141

Popping my dick free, Harmony smiles. "I was afraid real cocks weren't as big as the guy's in the movie. Like they used CGI to make it look so massive."

Before I can ask her to stop talking about giant porno cocks, Harmony cups my balls and gives them a squeeze while her mouth sucks vigorously at my erect dick.

I groan and reach for her hair. Wrapping her soft locks around my fist, I press her head down, wanting her to take more. How deep can she swallow my cock before she gags? I can't say the words aloud because my balls throb from her teasing fingers.

Harmony's throat relaxes enough for my cock to tease her tonsils. Groaning louder, I'm ready to jizz at the thought of her mouth stretched so far open for me. A turned-on Harmony strokes her pussy against my shin.

Never in my life have I wished to have a mirrored ceiling. I'd fucking love to see Harmony humping my leg while deep-throating me. One day, I need to convince her to let me videotape us. I'd enjoy admiring her pussy pre-and post-fuck.

I let loose into her throat, holding her still, forcing her to swallow everything she can take. Harmony could stop me at any time. All she needs to do is use her teasing fingers to apply a little pain to my balls. Instead, she sucks me dry before lifting her head and smiling at me with cum-drenched lips.

"I always dreamed of a man with a big cock. Now, I have one."

Tugging Harmony upward, I kiss her while my fingers search for her pussy. She clamps my hand between her thighs, startling me. Her lips leave mine, and her gaze darts to the door.

"Do you hear something?" she asks in a panicked tone. "Is that Keanu?"

"I don't hear shit," I reply, cupping her ass and having a good squeeze.

Tumbling off me, Harmony pushes away my hands. "I think he's crying."

"I'm telling you that I don't hear anything."

"You don't have a parent's hearing," she explains, searching the floor for her top. "Where is it?"

I climb out of bed, reach in my new dresser, and find her a shirt. "Wear one of mine."

Harmony catches the shirt and darts out of the room. Though I want to follow her, my boxers are shredded. I can't remember which damn drawer I shoved the others. By the time I get something on and walk across the condo to the second bedroom, I realize Harmony's parent hearing was right.

"The bed is big," Keanu says, hiccupping from crying. "I fall off."

Holding the boy against her while she rocks him, Harmony speaks in her soft, mommy voice that I find hypnotic. "No, you're okay. Mama was just talking to Dayton. I was right in the next room."

"It's too big. How I get down?"

"The steps are right here, baby, but we need to sleep."

"I want to go home."

Even before Harmony looks at me, I know she'll cave. Keanu's tone is too pathetic, and he's her baby, and I'd be a dick to make them stay.

"I'll get dressed, and we'll go to the trailer."

My tone isn't as pathetic as the kid's, but I know Harmony will cave with me, too. She's mine, and I'm sick of spending my nights without her.

"I'm sorry," she whispers while searching for her shoes. "He loves the room, but it's so much to adjust to."

"No more sleeping alone."

Harmony surprises me by bursting into laughter. "What will I do with my needy boys?"

I don't appreciate her laughing at me, but I guess giggling is better than her telling me no. I help Harmony locate her clothes along with their shoes.

Within fifteen minutes of my last orgasm and Keanu waking in a bed too big for his little head to wrap around, we're heading to her crappy little four-door car. I'll need to upgrade that soon.

Hell, I have an entire list of things I plan to soon change. I just hope Harmony takes to her new life better than the kid has so far.

THIRTY-SIX — HARMONY

Keanu is asleep about two minutes after climbing into his bed. He tells Carl they're home, and then he's out. I caress his little face before leaving the room and joining Dayton on the couch.

"What does this mean?" he asks.

"That you can't make a child sleep in a new place on the first try."

"Anything else?"

Dayton rests his left arm across the back of the couch and plays with my hair. I watch his face, searching for the insecurities his questions imply.

"Do you love me?" I ask instead.

"I already said I did."

"Say it again when we're not naked."

"I might love you more if you were naked."

Smiling, I lean my head back on the couch. "I'm not getting naked again tonight."

"Why not?"

"I'm tired, and I need to get up in a few hours."

"So am I, and so do I. But I could go for a round or two. Don't tell me you're weaker than a spoiled shit like me?"

"I feel no shame in wanting sleep."

Dayton studies me and then taps me on the back of the head. "You know, sweet Harmony, you have never said you loved me. So, you have some nerve expecting me to repeatedly proclaim my feelings for you."

"I did say it."

Dayton takes my hand and places it snugly over his dick hidden in jeans. "You have never ever said it. I know because I've been keeping track."

I think back to the last few days since he told me those three romantic little words. *Had I really not said them in return?*

"Well, you say it now, and I'll say it back."

"Nope," he says, standing up and walking to the bedroom.

I follow him like a sap, turning the lights off as I go. Dayton is a man capable of stripping naked in less than thirty seconds. By the time I finish brushing my teeth, he's stretched out in bed.

I stand in the dark bedroom and enjoy the way the moonlight shines off his hard muscles.

"I love you, Dayton."

"I don't believe you."

"If the only way to prove it is to fuck your brains out tonight, you're out of luck."

I change into night shorts and a tank top before joining him in bed. Dayton watches me until I'm resting on my side facing him.

"I do love you," I whisper.

"Just not enough to get spread eagle for me?"

"It's so close but just misses the mark."

Dayton smiles big in the dark. "I need a date for Bonn's wedding reception thing. You want to be my plus one?"

"I'm going to that, too, I think. Bonn's fiancée, what's her face, invited me. My kid, too."

"Huh? I didn't know you two were close," he says and yawns.

"I really like what you did with your condo."

"It's yours now, too. That's why the other room is set up for a kid. Not like I have a LEGO fetish."

"Keanu is warming up to you, but it takes time."

"You need to talk to him about that. Threaten him if necessary. I need him to wise up quick."

Giggling, I nudge his leg with my foot. "I would, but he cries, and I tend to back down."

"He's a tricky kid with that crying, ain't he?"

"Yeah, and his sweet little face."

Dayton stretches out even more. "He's got his mama's good looks. Lucky fucker."

"Are you comfortable?"

"As much as a man can get in this tiny oven you call home."

146

"You're hurting my feelings," I say, grinning as I close my eyes. "I might even cry."

"And I might even get you tissues if that happens. Oh, and fuck away your tears. I'll most definitely do that for you."

"I'm always impressed by the sacrifices you're willing to make for others."

Dayton's eyes close, but I catch him grinning. "Mom always said I was the kinder twin."

"It's sweet how much you love your mommy."

Laughing into the pillow, I don't see his expression. Yet, he reaches over and smacks my butt. I keep giggling long after his hand returns to his side of the bed. Once I fall silent, Dayton never speaks. I'm not sure which one of us crashes first, but I do know I doze off with a grin on my face.

THIRTY-SEVEN — DAYTON

Though I've never babysat before, I promise Harmony and Ruby that I can handle their kids while they go shopping. My woman fakes her trust less convincingly than her sister. Ruby probably thinks Chevelle will babysit me while I babysit them.

I decide fresh air will inspire Keanu to take a nap, and I really want him to sleep. He isn't normally a loud kid. However, he has the giggles today, and Chevelle keeps getting him going.

Now, they're on the jungle gym in the park next to the condo building. I stand nearby, arms crossed, making very clear how I don't want any of the moms or nannies talking to me. My gaze remains locked on my two small people as they play alone. They're as disinterested in the other kids as I am in the adults.

I hear a Harley pull into the lot where condo guests park. Glancing back, I see my father climbing off his hog and smoothing out his thick hair. He's such a diva about his 'do. I probably will be too at his age.

Focused on the kids again, I hope Mojo is looking for Camden, or maybe he's got a slut at the condo. Of course, my brother isn't home, and I'd know about any hookup hussy in my building. Nothing in Hickory Creek stays quiet for long.

"Hey, boy," Mojo says, patting me hard on the back. "We need to talk."

"Then talk."

"Inside."

"I can't leave," I say, gesturing with my chin toward Keanu and Chevelle in the sand.

Mojo looks at them for a long time. Eventually, I realize he doesn't know who the hell the kids belong to.

"You seriously don't recognize Howler's granddaughter?" I ask. "Bonn's kid, Chevelle."

Mojo gives me a dark frown. "What the hell is this?"

"I'm watching Chevelle and Harmony's son, Keanu. I know it looked like something completely different. That's why you're so confused by something others might find so obvious."

"You can never just say what you need to say."

"I don't think I was raised well. I mean, Mom did her best, but I didn't have a great male role model."

"What about Erik?"

"The man never speaks. I think he lost his tongue in the war."

"What war?"

Giving him a double shoulder shrug, I say, "I don't know. What possible wars can I choose from?"

"So, this is you now, huh? Playing the father to someone else's kid."

"Are you talking about Chevelle or Keanu?"

"You know what I'm talking about," he growls, losing his patience.

"Sometimes, a man needs to step into a family and take on the role of the missing parent. Erik did it with us. I'm doing it for Keanu."

"You're in a wonderful fucking mood."

"Well, maybe I feel emotionally attacked by your accusatory tone. You brought this on yourself with your bad attitude."

"I need to talk business."

"Then, you can come back later. Or you can wait until the kids are done playing."

"This is ridiculous," he says, walking away before turning back around. "I order you to take them inside now."

"Yes, sir. I should warn you that Keanu will cry loudly. Are you cool with that?"

Mojo sighs dramatically, sounding so pissed I nearly burst into laughter. *How close is he to yanking off his belt and giving me a whooping?*

"How long until they're done?"

"I don't know. Why don't you go ask them?"

"Why the fuck would...?"

149

"Language, Papa."

Around us, mothers, nannies, and that one stay-at-home father give us disapproving looks. I smirk in their direction, daring them to make a stink about my dad's dirty mouth.

"Give them ten minutes," I mutter after Mojo keeps eyeballing me.

"You shouldn't let your girlfriend push you into babysitting duty. Might as well hand over your balls at this rate."

"No offense, President, but I don't take romance advice from a man whose last real relationship was over twenty-five years ago with my mom."

"Boy, you're pissing on my last nerve."

"That's all I've ever wanted you to say, Daddy."

Mojo finally smiles. "You're such an ass. I blame your mother for spoiling you."

"You're thinking of Camden, who got spoiled. I've worked hard for everything I've ever gotten. That's why I have that huge chip on my handsome shoulder."

"I'm about ready to punch you in the head."

"In front of all these kids? Damn, I've heard old people lose their social skills. However, you're taking the shitting cake there."

I walk away from my father before he can reply. His anger entertains me. Yet, I'll need to zip it soon, or he really will punch me in the head. No way am I fucking up my babysitting duty by ending up with a concussion.

I squat down next to Keanu and Chevelle sitting in the sand. Harmony's little man grips Carl in his hand, and I'm relieved he hasn't lost the toy. Talk about another way to make me look like a crappy babysitter.

"See that guy?"

"Mojo?" Chevelle asks, surprising me by recognizing him.

"Yeah. That's my dad. He says I need to go inside in a few minutes, or he'll get mad, and I'll be in trouble."

Keanu kills me with his worried expression. His eyes widen, and he pats my arm. The kid is concerned about me.

150

If he weren't tiny, he'd probably promise to have my back against the giant biker man.

"For lunch, you can eat leftover pizza."

Chevelle smiles immediately. I immediately wonder if Ruby and Bonn are crappy parents who never feed their kid awesome fast food. *Ugh, I bet they have salad for dinner.* That would explain how Bonn looks like a male pinup model rather than a real man like me.

"Can we go now?" Chevelle asks.

"No. I need to make my dad wait. He's been bad, so this is his punishment."

Keanu's dark eyes stare holes into Mojo's face until the old man walks away. Smiling, I can't get over the kid's impressively intimidating gaze.

After making my father wait five minutes, I lead the kids inside the condo building. Mojo grunts with disapproval when he enters my place and sees the work I had done. Though his reaction makes me smile. I keep my big mouth shut until the kids are settled next to the living room coffee table. Hands and faces washed, they stare at the TV and eat without saying a word.

"What do you want?" I ask my dad.

"How's JJ?"

"Fine, I guess. I'm not with him right now."

"Stop being a twat."

"Stop acting like I live up JJ's ass."

"I need to know what he's up to."

"Why now when he's been up to shit for fucking months?"

Mojo shrugs before sticking his head in my fridge to find a beer. Opening the bottle, he shrugs again.

"What do you want me to say? I thought he might be a good kid and work out. Howler liked him."

"Bonn says Howler's going through a midlife crisis. Sounds about right. Aren't you two the same age?"

My father takes a few swigs from his beer and then glances at the kids. "Has Bonn said anything about how Common Bend is going?"

"No."

"Would you tell me if he did?"

"Yeah. That's why he doesn't tell me and Cam shit about his business."

Nodding, Mojo takes another swig. "I don't want JJ in the club."

"Then don't let him in."

"Howler is already talking like JJ's been patched in."

"And you came here for my advice?"

"Maybe."

"Stop worrying so damn much. The more you worry, the more JJ worries. Give him enough rope, and the guy will hang himself. Right now, you're on edge, and he senses it. Not a good way to get him to fuck up."

"Did he tell you that?"

"How did you ever become president if you're this stupid?" I ask and then duck when Mojo takes a swing at me. Laughing, I back away. "I ask as your son and not one of your minions."

"You're cruising for a bruising, boy," he growls, still coming after me.

"Keanu, whatcha watching?"

The kid turns toward us, sees Mojo, and locks onto my father with that dark gaze of his. For whatever reason, Mojo can't handle the kid watching him and immediately heads to the front door.

"You're leaving?" I ask, following after him. "After giving me shit and making us come inside, now you're leaving after talking to me for five minutes?" When Mojo frowns back at me, I smile. "No, wait, you're right. You should go."

"You're an asshole."

"So are you. What's your point?"

"You better tell me if you get info on JJ."

"I will. Just like I would if I got info on Bonn or anyone else who might harm the club. What's your fucking point?"

"I like you better when you're drunk."

"Don't we all," I say, shutting the door on him.

Back on the floor, Chevelle watches TV while Keanu focuses on me.

"He's gone," he says, climbing onto the couch to see me better.

"Yeah. He's a meanie."

Keanu sighs dramatically, and I struggle not to laugh. He's so serious about Mojo getting me in trouble. The kid cares about my happiness, and I realize I care about him, too. Not just because he's Harmony's boy, either.

My fingers caress his thick black hair like his mom often does. This little man owns Harmony's big heart. Sometimes, I feel lucky to fit anywhere in her life when Keanu takes up so much of it.

Right now, I want him to know I appreciate how he has my back. Like his mama, Keanu doesn't care about my money or power. He likes me—Dayton—not just one of the Rutgers twins. The truth is few people actually prefer me to Camden. That's why I'll protect those who see past my bullshit to the real man underneath. Now, Keanu's a member of that very short list.

THIRTY-EIGHT — HARMONY

Ruby doesn't enjoy dressing up. For her wedding, she'd rather wear jeans and a nice blouse than a fancy dress. Still, she has Daisy and me meet her at a bridal shop to look at gowns.

"I wouldn't mind something low-key," Ruby says, passing the white gowns and stopping by the bridesmaid's dresses. "Something a little fancy, but nothing like those."

I look at the gowns Ruby gestures at, finding them too grandiose. I can't even imagine how much they cost either.

Daisy hums to a song only she can hear, but I think it's "She Bop" by Cyndi Lauper.

"I love Dayton," I announce once we start rifling through the second rack.

Nodding, my sisters smile in unison.

"The trifecta has finally occurred," Daisy says.

"What?"

"The three Hallstead men with the three Slater women. Now, we can live in the condo building together, just like we did at Lush Gardens."

"I'm not ready to move yet."

"So, like in a week, then?" Daisy pushes while wearing a grin.

"Maybe. Dayton has revamped his entire place. You should see the room he set up for Keanu. It's a million times more amazing than anything I'd ever come up with."

My sisters sigh "aw" in unison.

"So, what's the holdup?" Ruby asks.

"There's no holdup."

"Then, why do you look less than thrilled?"

Shrugging, I search the rack of dresses. "I thought falling in love would feel different."

"Different how?" Daisy asks.

"I thought falling in love would be a big moment punching me in the gut. Instead, it crept up on me until it just was there."

"So, you're disappointed?"

"No. I'm just surprised," I say, avoiding their gazes. "I never realized I loved Dayton until he mentioned I hadn't said anything. The entire relationship happened so fast. One minute, I was hardcore crushing on him. Then, we were just messing around. Next, he was changing his condo and talking about love. I should have thought I wasn't ready, but I feel him in here," I say, patting my chest. "When he acts like a dumbass, I don't hate him. I just think he's *my* dumbass."

"Is he a dumbass a lot?" Ruby asks.

"No, not really. Dayton's a chill guy. He mostly complains the trailer is too small and has no air conditioning."

"So, has he asked you to move in?"

"No, or maybe yes. Dayton doesn't tend to blurt things out. He talks about stuff in a roundabout way. That's fine, too. I don't enjoy heartfelt therapy sessions with men."

Daisy stops fiddling with dresses and nuzzles against me. "I don't think Dayton's said more than a few sentences to me for the entire time I've been married to Camden. I sometimes forget he talks about anything besides pussy and booze."

Daisy flinches when she realizes what she said aloud in a public place. I grin at her embarrassed expression.

Ruby shows me a dress and raises an eyebrow. "What about this one?"

"Sure," I say, not caring what I wear.

Daisy shakes her head, though. "I'm short, remember? You tall chicks can wear something poofy without looking like you have a huge butt. Me, not so much."

"It's not poofy."

"Whatever, tall sister," Daisy mutters, frowning at Ruby.

"I guess I could elope like you did with Camden. No dress necessary for that."

155

"Don't copy me," Daisy says, patting Ruby's shoulder. "Be your own person."

While they share a smile, my mind is stuck on Dayton. Even if my sisters picked a lime green mini dress with rhinestones, I'd only nod approvingly.

"Don't hide in your head, hippy," Daisy says, stroking my hair. "If something's bothering you, spill it."

Shaking my head, I keep looking at the dresses. The words I need escape me. No way can I put my feelings into a coherent sentence.

Leaving the bridal shop without buying anything, we stop for lunch at the soup and salad restaurant.

"When I first held Keanu," I explain after sitting silently while people around us talk about salad toppings, "I was so overwhelmed with my love for him. I could barely breathe. I'd loved him before then, but it was different. Once he was in my arms, I was bowled over with emotion."

"He was a cute baby," Daisy says, dumping more bacon on her salad.

"But what if I don't love Dayton enough?" I ask, finally finding the words to explain my feelings. "I haven't had that punch in the gut realization with him. I kept thinking I loved him in an easy way. Like, we were just meant to be, so I don't need to be overwhelmed with the feeling. But what if I'm wrong? What if I love him in a lazy way? Is that enough? Is he settling for someone who doesn't love him in that 'crazy, tearing her hair out, humping his leg all the time' way?"

"Who do you know who acted that way when they fell in love?"

We both stare at Daisy, who shrugs. "I didn't tear my hair out."

"Still, you were floating around like a person who'd changed because of finding her man. I'm the same person I was."

"I didn't change that much. Camden just gave me confidence. You didn't need that from Dayton."

"I feel like my love isn't good enough for him. I should be drooling over him and—"

"Nope," Ruby interrupts. "That's not how it works."

"Yeah, I never drooled," Daisy adds.

"Listen, Harmony," Ruby says, staring me in the eyes. "You're a working mom. The stuff you're talking about is teenage girl crap. You might not stare dreamily at Dayton and write his name on your notebook, but you understand him when most people don't. Even Camden doesn't get his brother. You get him, and he gets you. That's what matters. Not the fireworks crap."

"Well, there are fireworks in bed. Otherwise, I worry we're too chill. Boring even."

"If he isn't complaining, why are you worried?"

The hot tears spilling from my eyes surprise me. "I don't know."

When Ruby hands me a napkin, I quickly wipe away the tears.

"Dayton is special," I whisper. "I want him to have the best. I'm not sure my laidback kind of love is enough. I feel like I've let him down by not going gaga like I did with Keanu."

"Well, first off, you need to stop comparing your feelings for your son to your feelings for a man. Keanu is completely dependent on you. Dayton isn't. Keanu has been your main concern for four years. Loving Dayton is new. He's still learning to fit you into his life and you in his."

Nodding, Daisy takes my hand. "You're so good at taking care of people, but you don't need to take care of Dayton. He's a grown man and perfectly capable of living without you. He's choosing to be with you because he has great taste. He doesn't need you to do anything besides be yourself."

Even knowing they're right, I struggle against my insecurities. Keanu isn't the only one stressed about change. I lost Daisy to Camden. My former client died. Ruby and Elle moved away. I started a new job. And then, there's Dayton. I worry the changes left me failing with the important stuff.

"I don't like letting people down, and I feel like I am with Dayton."

"Have you talked to him about it?"

"No."

Ruby's hand shoos Daisy's away from mine and takes its place. "Is it possible you're building up a problem in your head that doesn't exist?"

"Yes."

We smile at my honesty and return to our salads. Though I'm still emotional, sharing my fears aloud did help some. Hearing my sisters tell me what I logically knew helped even more.

THIRTY-NINE — DAYTON

Watching Keanu sleep on his face, I wonder if I need to flip him over. I remember Mom saying something years ago about not letting Hudson sleep on his stomach. Of course, my little brother was a baby. *When are people old enough to sleep face down without dying?*

Chevelle sleeps on her back, making me worry more. She's seven, so if she's doing it, shouldn't Keanu? I'm ready to walk into the room and roll him over when I hear the key in the door and know Harmony is home.

"I love you," she blurts out when she sees me.

"I know. Thanks, but can he sleep on his face like that?" I say, tugging her to the bedroom and pointing at Keanu. "You didn't leave any rules about sleeping. So, if he dies, that's on you."

Harmony smirks and pulls me out of the room. "He's fine. Thank you for keeping him alive."

"I fed him and washed his hands. I'm pretty much a fucking natural at this."

Her smile widens as she tugs at my shirt. "You did fantastic for a newbie."

"Yeah, I did. I also managed that while my dad visited to give me grief. If the kid mentions a scary man, he means Mojo."

"What did he want?" Harmony asks, giving me a sexy frown.

"He's an old man worried he's lost control of his empire. The minute Camden got stupid over Daisy, my father's been in a spiral of pussification."

"Did you tell him that?" she asks, wrapping her arms around my waist.

"No. I was really polite. He *is* my club president, after all."

Harmony lifts onto her tippy-toes and puckers up. I don't kiss her, though.

"If you're thinking about fucking, I can't right now. I'm babysitting your kid."

"I'm here," she says and then smirks. "You're messing with me."

"Not even a little. Something happened today between the boy and me. Now, I take my job very seriously."

"What?"

I shrug, feeling on the spot. I reach down and give her ass a double cheek squeeze. Harmony wraps me tighter in her arms.

"We didn't pick out anything to wear today," she says. "Ruby wants to wear something simple. She's also cheap about clothes for herself."

"I love Keanu," I blurt out. "That happened today. I realized it, anyway. I thought I just cared about him because he's yours. However, I love the little bastard, which makes me edgy. Maybe we should have a quickie."

"They'll wake up the very second you drop your pants. It's the universe's way of messing with us."

"Are you gonna respond to what I said?"

Harmony smiles sweetly at me. "Well, of course, you love Keanu. He's a wonderful kid, and you have a good heart."

"You make me sound like a wuss. After seeing my father act like a pussy, I don't want to become one, too."

"There's nothing weak about loving those who deserve loving."

"No, there isn't," I say, relaxing just a little.

"You don't seem convinced."

"My father used to seem indestructible. Now, he's edgy and fears he's losing control of the club. He isn't, though. Just thinking he's weak made him weak. What if worrying about you and Keanu turns me soft? Weakness begins with a single idea. Then, it builds until becoming capable of taking down men who should know better."

"A midlife crisis can make a strong man weak. However, you're not having a midlife crisis."

"I'm aware I'm not an old man grasping at his former glory, but thanks for pointing that out," I say, letting her go and walking to the bedroom.

Harmony follows, wearing a concerned expression. I wait until she's in the room before I shut the door and lock it.

"Drop your pants and let's have a quickie. I changed my mind."

Harmony's pale green eyes widen. "But the kids," she says, even while reaching for the band on her sweatpants.

"I have this radio thing." Turning up the sound on the baby monitor, I show it to her. "If they so much as fart, we'll hear it."

Harmony looks at the monitor and reaches into her shirt. Ten seconds later, she pops her bra-free and shows it to me.

"Just a quickie. Now drop your pants."

Grinning, I hand her the monitor and lean her over the bed. Her pants come down with an easy motion. Mine soon follow. I press my cock against her pink flesh and find her hot but not wet.

"What's a guy gotta do to make you dripping wet?"

"Give me a shower?" she teases, glancing back at me. "Or I have two nipples that wouldn't mind some attention if you think that would be easier."

Leaning forward, I slide my hands under her thin pink shirt until I find those waiting nipples. The moment I graze her hard flesh, Harmony shivers and wiggles her butt. My dick twitches at the feel of her.

"Are you ready now?" I whisper in her ear while kneading her nipples into hard tips.

"No, I need more."

"I need to fuck you before the kids ruin my hard-on."

"Then, fuck me, but don't stop touching my breasts. That feels so good."

My dick responds to her words by seeking out the heat of her pussy. She's not super wet when I thrust into her the first time. Or the second. By the third, Harmony's face down on the bed, moaning into the mattress.

"That didn't take much," I murmur, smiling at her reaction. "Were you walking around all day waiting for this moment?"

Harmony nods slightly. Yet, she only looks up long enough to check the monitor. Finding it quiet, she returns to moaning and saying my name.

"Your pussy is on fire," I groan, thrusting harder. "I keep forgetting how good it feels. Maybe I am having a midlife crisis, and my memory is the first thing to go."

Harmony muffles her laughter before her voice returns to loud moans against the mattress. I pinch her nipples harder, wanting her to come so I can. Then, we can get our pants on before the kids ruin the party. If not for their impressionable little minds, I'd fuck this woman for another hour. Not wanting to pay their future therapy bills, I use my thumbs to taunt the shit out of her nipples until Harmony shoves her ass back and comes hard around my cock.

Jizzing deep inside my still groaning woman is the best reward for a well-done babysitting job.

FORTY — HARMONY

La Famiglia's grand opening is a big deal in Hickory Creek Township. The local paper covers the event, interviewing Mom and Ruby and the restaurant's investors— the Hallstead sisters. With all the hoopla, Dayton refuses to go anywhere near La Famiglia. Well, until Keanu asks him to come along with us.

My boy suddenly has the power to bend a powerful man to his will. I'm admittedly a little jealous of Keanu's gift.

"I don't want to mingle," Dayton says during the drive. "I refuse to bond with my mom or aunts. I don't want to eat anything weird. I might stay in the SUV."

"Keanu, should Dayton stay in the SUV?" I ask, glancing back at him in his car seat.

"No. It's hot in here."

"It's hot in the trailer," Dayton points out, "and you still like it there."

"Yes."

A frowning Dayton glances at me. "Did I win that argument or not?"

"No, he did."

"How?"

"He's three, and that defeats logic."

"Fine, but I will not mingle. Or smile. This thing is lame, and I won't actively participate."

Laughing, I poke his muscled arm. "Why are you so tense?"

"I don't know. I got a bad feeling about this."

My smile disappears immediately. "Bad feeling like something dangerous could happen or like you might be annoyed by someone?"

"Both," Dayton says and then sighs. "I don't know. La Famiglia is a sensitive subject with the club, especially with Howler and Mojo."

"And JJ," I quietly add.

163

"Yeah, him."

"Should I worry?"

"No. You ought to smile and talk chick stuff with your sisters. Keanu can play with Elle. I'll do all the worrying."

"Meatballs!" Keanu yells and waves his arms around.

I smile back at him, only to find he's talking to Carl about food.

"The kid digs his meatballs," Dayton says, smirking. "I wonder if that means he's gay."

"Maybe. Ask me again in ten years."

"Will do."

We arrive at the restaurant to find the parking lot full and a line of people outside waiting to get in. Dayton drops off Keanu and me before leaving us to find a spot down the street.

Inside the kid-friendly Italian restaurant, Ruby hurries from one table to another, making sure everyone is happy. She smiles and nods and smiles more. She's clearly overwhelmed.

Nearby, Bonn and Elle draw on the chalkboard walls. Keanu sees his cousin and tugs at my hand so we can join them. Once he's safely under Bonn's care, I push through the crowd of people to reach Ruby.

"Congrats," I say, hugging her and maneuvering us away from a table full of shamelessly loud kids.

"It's so busy," she says over the noise. "I didn't think it would be quite this packed right off the bat."

"People are excited about something new, and you gave them a cool place to try."

"I'm glad you came."

"But we should leave soon and free up a table?"

Ruby grins. "You read my mind. Take Bonn and Elle with you."

"Well, Keanu won't leave until he gets meatballs. See if you can make that happen, and we'll get out of your hair."

Hugging me again, Ruby doesn't want to let go, even if she knows people are waiting for her attention. I spot two waitresses looking overly confused, plus a table full of cranky children ready to set the world on fire with their screams.

I walk back outside to find Dayton. Glancing around, I notice the Hallstead sisters speaking to people waiting in line. Fear ripples up my spine because I don't want to talk to Dayton's mom tonight. Though she's a nice woman who loves her sons, Clara's also powerful and scary.

Spotting another terrifying person, I notice JJ noticing me noticing him. He stops talking to Dayton, who is focused on the ground. I consider walking inside. Yet, something draws me toward the men.

"Once Keanu gets his food, we should probably head out," I say before Dayton even seems to notice me.

My guy nods and reaches his arm out for me to get closer. I smile at JJ, who does not return the gesture.

"Am I interrupting?" I ask Dayton.

Wrapping a lock of blond hair behind his ear, he shrugs in a way that reminds me of Keanu.

"JJ was wondering if he wanted to deal with the mayhem inside. I told him no, so we're standing out here where it's safe."

"Smart, but Ruby is kicking us out soon. She needs the free tables for everyone waiting in line."

"Where's the kid?"

"With Elle and Bonn," I say and then add, "They need to leave soon, too. Maybe they can come back to the condo, so the kids can keep playing."

I notice JJ's jaw twitch when I mention Bonn's name. Dayton probably picks up on it, too. However, his expression is unreadable. If I didn't know him, I'd guess he was thinking about food or bowel movements.

"I could go for a beer," Dayton says since booze is his safe topic whenever on the spot. "I'm surprised more parents don't drink heavily."

Rolling my eyes, I step away from the men and take Dayton's hand. "We need to get going. You're more than welcome to come along, JJ."

Dayton doesn't react, but I know he does *not* want this man around Keanu and me. I'm also aware JJ has no interest in spending time with Bonn or the kids.

Still, I play along as if JJ is part of our circle. That's the lie Dayton's been selling for months. Since we're a team now, I need to lie, too.

"Naw, that's cool. I have plans," JJ says, never looking at me as his gaze focuses hard on Dayton.

"I'll see you tomorrow at the site."

JJ frowns harder at Dayton, who stares at the street lights as if he's already downed a kegger. I don't know why I find his fake stoned look so sexy. Yet, I'm tempted to ask Bonn to watch Keanu for a few hours, so I can ride this lying sex-machine.

After JJ walks across the street to his Harley, Dayton tugs me toward the restaurant.

"What was that?" I whisper.

"He's pissed about the restaurant. Might even be thinking about burning it down again. If anyone asks, though, you didn't hear that from me."

"Please, don't let him burn down La Famiglia after Ruby and Mom worked so hard on it."

Dayton shakes his head. "Don't forget my mom and aunts worked hard, too."

"Sure, if you consider writing checks and calling in favors hard. Then, yeah, they worked their butts off."

"Don't make this a class war thing," he says, wrapping an arm around my shoulders. "They worked in their own way."

"Does that mean you'll make sure nothing happens?"

"Why does everyone think I have my hand shoved up JJ's ass and control his every fucking move?"

I stop walking as we reach the front door. "Dayton, I love your dirty mouth. However, you need to shut that shit off once we're surrounded by children."

"No."

Grinning, I shove him back against the wall. "Stay here. I'll be right back with Keanu and his meatballs."

"Shit, if we're leaving already, I'll get the car."

166

I glance around his wide shoulder to check if JJ is gone. Seeing his Harley's backlight flashing in the distance instantly calms me. The Brotherhood never scared me, though I always remained wary. Yet, JJ is too close to Dayton, and his enemies include Bonn.

The sooner the asshole goes away permanently, the better.

FORTY-ONE — DAYTON

Likely hearing through the rumor mill that Harmony's nearly moved into my place, Mom decides she must meet my woman and Keanu before Bonn's wedding. Her initial plan is for us to visit her big house, where she'll cook a lavish meal and show off her wealth. Nothing intimidates people more than the size of Mom's bank account, and she's able to scare them while wearing a smile.

When Camden and Daisy eloped, Mom threw a party at my aunt Alice's house. After all, she has a rule about my father never entering her home. I don't blame her. Dad seems to regularly step in dog shit, and the man refuses to wipe his feet.

Making a preemptive move, I invite her to my condo for dinner. No fancy shit. If Mom insists on intimidating Harmony, she'll need to do it in a more obvious way.

I open the door to welcome Mom, Erik, and Hudson into my renovated condo.

"I brought pie," she says, smiling so big I bet her face hurts.

Taking the dessert, I kiss the top of her head and gesture hello to my step-dad and brother.

"I ordered dinner."

Though Mom opens her mouth to ask what we're having, she stops herself. I smile at her expression, and she gives me a smirk knowing I'm onto her.

"Place looks good," Erik says, walking into the condo and searching for a weakness in my security.

I frown at how he cannot turn off the soldier part of his brain. Hudson follows the sound of Keanu's voice and peers into the second room.

"No wonder you talk so much," I tell Mom while setting the pie on the stove. "You live in a house with two silent men."

"They talk plenty," Mom lies as her gaze takes in the condo's changes. "You installed carpet," she says, walking into the living room. "I didn't realize anyone wanted carpet anymore."

"Keanu runs around and falls down and does other three-year-old stuff. I figured he'd get less injured on the carpet. It's also what he's used to at the trailer."

Mom stops looking around and stares at me. "Did Harmony suggest the carpet?"

"Asking her for ideas would have ruined my surprise."

"My boy," Mom says, cupping my face. "You're growing into quite the man."

"I'm thirty-three."

Mom pulls me down for a hug. "You thinking about that child is real sweet, honey."

"He's my woman's kid. That makes him my responsibility."

Mom laughs. "You and Cam are so much alike. Never occurred to either of you to have a serious girlfriend before jumping right into the 'my woman' territory."

"We might be alike, but I'm still better."

Mom pats my cheek before focusing on an approaching Harmony. The women smile and say hello. They're both nervous. Each one suffers a preconceived view about the other.

Studying them, I wonder if Harmony's appeal really is that she reminds me of my blonde mother. If so, is that a good or bad thing? One woman is dressed in a hundred-dollar well-fitting beige dress with shoes costing twice that much. The other wears a flowery yellow skirt and a white tank she likely bought at the thrift store. They don't seem much alike besides their hair color.

"I ordered Korean for dinner," I announce. "It was that or pizza, and I had pizza for breakfast."

Mom flashes an amused smirk while Harmony narrows her eyes at me. In her mind, I should make this visit as calm as possible. As I see it, I need to set down my foot with my mother's meddling now, so it doesn't continue for the rest of my life.

I already see Mom bugging me about grandkids and whose place we'll visit during the holidays. A naturally competitive woman, she'll insist on beating Sally Slater at every turn in the future.

"Does Keanu speak Korean?" Mom asks Harmony.

And so it begins...

"Yes, some. I'm teaching him. Then, he can speak to his grandparents in South Korea. They're learning English, too. Pretty soon, our conversations will last more than a few minutes with Keanu mostly saying hello and waving."

"Where is he now?"

"In his room," I answer, giving a head nod toward where Hudson keeps watch.

Mom walks to the second bedroom, and Harmony starts to follow until I grab her shirt.

"Watch her. She's in a mood."

Harmony nods. "I can tell. All the smiling and friendliness was a dead giveaway."

Kissing her forehead, my lips then slip down her temple to her cheek before sliding to her ear.

"My mother is a wonderful woman, and I love her dearly. However, she's also a bitch who will challenge you forever if you don't pass her tests right away."

"Did she test Daisy?"

"I assume. You know I don't care about other people's problems."

"Since when?"

"Since I have a family to worry about now. No one else matters."

"Except your club," she says, poking me in the gut. "Oh, and your mommy and brothers and probably your father and Erik."

"I don't know about the last two. They can worry about themselves."

"Oh, and you care about Bonn and Elle."

"Shut up, will ya? I tried to make a point about me being fierce for my family. Why go shit all over it with logic and facts?"

170

When I give her a dark frown, Harmony scowls right back at me. There's no time for a contest, but I don't think I'd win with her fingers teasing under my shirt.

"Geez, woman, my mom is in the next room," I say, walking past her with a quick smack to her ass.

Harmony chases after me and slaps my butt before we enter the room.

"What do you have in your hand?" Mom asks Keanu.

"Carl. A dog chewed his face, but he can still play."

I think back to how silly his Carl issue seemed just weeks ago. Now, I'd kill to protect that toy. *I guess that means love has changed me for the better.*

FORTY-TWO — HARMONY

People have always had their own ideas about who I am. *Trailer trash. The bastard child of a ski bum and a party girl. A hippy. Single mom. A lush like her mama.* That last one came from the losers at the Red Barn Bar.

No matter what they say, I don't let it faze me. After all, I only get one life, and pleasing others won't change that fact.

Yet, a part of me wants Clara's approval. Dayton is as much a mama's boy as a man can be without having her wipe his ass for him. That means her opinion matters to me like most people's never will.

So, when she stands in Keanu's room, I start worrying about gaining her approval. Even worse, I care about how she sees Keanu. *Is he well-behaved enough for her liking? Does she look down at his used clothes? Is she judging my mothering skills?*

Then, Keanu's dark-eyed gaze finds me, and he smiles. His love erases my worries. As long as I do right by him, people can think whatever they want about what kind of mother I am.

"Is Keanu a Korean name?" Clara asks, sitting on his bed.

"No, it's Hawaiian, but his middle name is Ji-Hoon after his father."

Nodding and smiling, Clara seems like the nicest person in the world, but I have no clue what she's thinking. *Am I a hussy trapping her boozehound son into a relationship? Is Dayton only hooking up with me because Camden nailed down my sister? Or is she thinking something I can't even imagine?*

"What name would you have chosen for a girl?" she asks, and I'm startled by the question.

After a moment, I blurt out, "Calypso."

"That's a sweet name," she lies.

"I'd still use it if I got pregnant with a girl. Not sure about another son's name. Maybe Aesop."

Clara's smile never wavers, making me think I could pick any silly name in the universe without her so much as flinching.

"I always wanted a daughter," she says. "But boys are fun."

Glancing back to the door, I notice Hudson is gone. Dayton now stands in his place.

"Are you okay?" I ask, startled by his enraged expression.

"Mom, can you watch the kid for a second while I talk to Harmony about something?"

Clara doesn't finish saying yes before Dayton pulls me out of the room. Holding my hand, he tugs me across the living room and into his bedroom, where he shuts the door.

"What?" I cry, yanking my hand free.

"I don't like kids."

My panic at his anger shifts into confusion. "I don't know how to respond to that."

"I hate the crying and the smell. They stink, you know?" he says, pacing around the room. "I can't stand their little fingers on everything and how they don't wipe their noses. And even their good smells are gross."

"Okay," I say, crossing my arms and gritting my teeth.

Dayton notices my tension and reacts by running his hands through his hair. Normally, this gesture signals he's decompressing. However, I don't know what to think right now.

"But I love Keanu," Dayton says, taking a step closer and caressing my cheek. "So, maybe if you really want to have another kid... I mean, one with me, then I could learn to get over the issues I have with their stink."

"Why are you freaking out about this now?"

"Mom was asking about names. She's already gotten babies on the brain. Soon, you will too. Then, I'll need to deal with baby crap. Not that I wouldn't figure it out if that's what you want. However, it's not really what I want. Not yet, anyway. Does that make sense?"

"Oh, Dayton, you big dumb sexy idiot," I say, cupping his face. "I don't want another baby right now."

"You don't?"

"No. I'm already busy with a job I love. I want to give all my free time to you and Keanu. Any leftover time goes to my family and occasionally myself. Another baby doesn't make sense right now."

"Oh."

"Are you disappointed?" I tease while resting my head against his chest.

"No, but that might change when Camden starts pounding out kids with Daisy. Everyone will no doubt ask when I plan to do the same."

Staring up at him, I frown. "I refuse to have more kids so that you can compete with your brother."

"No, that's probably not a good plan. Kids are a lot of work, and they smell."

"Stop saying Keanu smells," I mutter, letting go of Dayton's hard, hot body.

"Not him. He's a good kid. I guess ours would be, too. However, I really hate everyone else's kids."

"What about Elle?"

"I could do without all her dolls and princess crap. Otherwise, she's good."

"Yeah, you're not ready for another kid," I say and then hug him. "But neither am I. My mom did a good job loving my sisters and me at the same time. Yet, I worry I'll give Keanu too little if I have another kid. Also, I don't think I could keep my current position if I were pregnant. My clients get aggressive sometimes. So, I'm not ready, and I don't see that changing for a few years, at least."

"Good."

"Do you feel better now?" I ask, pulling him down so I can nuzzle his throat with my lips.

"Yes."

"You don't think all those negative things about Keanu, do you?"

"No, but I wasn't around for the diapers and baby crying parts."

"And you haven't seen him throw a massive tantrum yet. That'll be fun."

"I'll let you handle that while I go out and get a pack of smokes."

Rolling my eyes, I walk to the door. "You pull that shit, and I'll shove those smokes up your ass."

"Kinky," he says, following close behind me as we leave the room.

I take his hand and squeeze it reassuringly. Despite his cocky stance, he's allowed his mom's presence and her hopes for him to get under his skin. Undoubtedly, life was easier when he spent his days drunk, and every word coming out of his mouth was a lie. Now, he's responsible for two other people's happiness and being the best version of himself.

FORTY-THREE — DAYTON

Somehow, Camden beats me to Bonn's office. He was probably in White Horse when he got the message from Daisy, who works in the town. I'd been eating pie at Mom's when Harmony texted me. Camden only won by default, but his triumph still gnaws at my ego.

Arriving at Bonn's office in Common Bend, I park next to Camden's Harley and head inside. I step through the shattered front door, ignoring the glass crunching under my boots.

"Anyone dead?" I ask Bonn.

"Why are you here?"

From his tone, I suspect he said something similar to Camden. My brother frowns at me and then back at Bonn.

"If someone takes a shot at family," Camden growls, "you come to see if they're okay."

Nodding, I gesture at Camden. "What he said, but my version would have sounded tougher and less whiny."

"Shut up."

"So, let me get this straight," Bonn says, crossing his massive arms. "I called Ruby to tell her what happened. Then, she instantly informed her sisters, who instantly informed you two. Is that right?"

Camden and I nod in unison, causing Bonn to sigh loudly. "I pissed off a lot of people when I helped Angus Hayes take over Common Bend. Someone was bound to send me a warning."

"Was it a warning?" I ask and walk to the front door. "Or did they have a real shot at hitting someone?"

"I was at the door when they fired."

Camden exhales hard. "That's not a message. They were trying to put you six feet under."

"Bonn, I get you're a big boy, and you don't want anyone changing your diapers. However, you're acting like a little bitch right now."

"How do you figure, smart guy?" Bonn asks, crossing his arms again.

"Someone took a shot at you today," I explain patiently. "You, a family man with a kid at home and who's soon to be married. Yet, you act like our concern is silly shit. I think you're downplaying things you shouldn't. This is why I'm considered the smart guy in our group."

Bonn exhales slowly and unclenches his arms. "I don't want to make a big shit about it. Not with Ruby already terrified."

"She isn't here. You can be square with us."

"Fine then. Someone took a shot at me, and the list of suspects is fucking long."

"We can help you narrow it down," Camden offers.

"I don't know if he'll be cool with that."

Before we can ask who Bonn means, we hear Angus Hayes coming through the shattered front door. The giant man puffs on a cigar like an enraged locomotive, making me want to laugh in his big fucking face. I don't, of course. But it's a tough call.

"They come here to fucking confess?" he asks Bonn.

Camden shakes his head. "We came as a family concerned about one of our own."

"Well, riddle me this, fucker. How do I know it wasn't one of your fucking people who took a shot at one of my fucking people?"

"I only heard the word 'fuck.' Is he coming onto me?" I ask Camden.

Hayes growls in my direction. "Don't start with me, Twin Number Two."

"I prefer Turd Twin, but what-fucking-ever."

"None of our people have any reason to mess with Bonn," Camden says, ignoring my attempt to start trouble.

"He's running my shit in a fucking place your twat nugget fathers wanted to run. Don't sell me bullshit about your club's clean hands."

"Our guys aren't fucking with your shit. If we wanted to take a shot at your organization, we'd aim for the top."

"I thought you two had an agreement," I say, gesturing between Camden and Hayes. "Or did I hear that wrong?"

"You told him?" Hayes growls at my brother.

Camden shrugs. "The idiot's a troublemaker. If I want him to behave, he needs to know the rules."

"I'm all about the rules," I admit, smiling despite the men's bad moods.

"The Brotherhood didn't do this," Camden states as a fact.

Hayes gives my brother a nasty frown, but Camden doesn't relent. He believes with all his precious heart that no one in the Brotherhood would go against the wishes of our illustrious president and VP. Camden's fucking naïve to think a particular wannabe club brother wouldn't pull this move.

JJ mentions Common Bend every time I see him. Mainly how his half-brother stole the town from their father, Howler. If JJ got it in his fat head to deal with the problem, he would have no problem killing Bonn.

He's also a terrible shot, so missing so badly is completely in the fucker's wheelhouse.

I don't share these thoughts with Camden or Bonn and certainly not with Hayes. I'm unsure if I should tell anyone my suspicions or what I plan to do about it. Camden might need his hands clean for when he runs the Brotherhood, and Bonn's allegiance is to a man considered—at best—the club's friendly enemy.

There's only one person I can trust with my secrets. However, I'm not sure she has the stomach to hear them.

FORTY-FOUR — HARMONY

Ruby doesn't even pretend she's calm when I arrive at the condo with Keanu. Daisy runs into the hallway and directs us to Ruby's place. Elle immediately takes her cousin to the living room for TV and snacks.

I hug Ruby, who is downing a pint of ice cream.

"He could have died," she whispers.

Though Daisy nods, her jaw is so tight I'm worried she'll break her teeth. "But, he didn't."

I place my hands over theirs and squeeze. "I love you both, and I know you love your guys. I love Dayton, too. Yet, this is the life we've signed onto, and we need to be strong now."

"Is it really that simple?" Ruby asks.

"No, but we need to make it seem that way for our men. This thing will rattle them. It's our job to give them back their confidence by faking like we're confident, too."

"I don't think we're supposed to lie in a marriage," Daisy says.

As we laugh at the thought of always telling the truth, I notice their tension fades the tiniest bit.

"I'm not saying we shouldn't worry. Still, Howler and Mojo stayed alive all these years. Neither one is a Mensa member."

"It's a different time," Ruby says before shoving another scoop of ice cream in her mouth.

"Is it really, though? Or does it seem scarier now because we see the situation from the inside rather than from the outside?" I ask, trying to stay rational rather than worrying over where Dayton might be right this moment.

Ruby sighs. "Bonn will know I'm full of shit if he comes home and I act cool with someone trying to kill him."

"Camden always knows when I'm lying," Daisy adds.

"You two are so lame. I lie to Dayton constantly, just to keep him on his toes."

"Really?" Daisy asks, giving me an unconvinced frown.

"No, but it's not so difficult to lie. Or at least fudge the truth. Ask Bonn if he has it handled rather than drilling him for details. When Camden mentions it, Daisy, you can say he better find out who it was and handle the problem. That way, the guys will reassure us about how manly they are and how they can beat down any threat."

Ruby and Daisy look at each other and sigh in unison. I wish I were in on their internal musing. Instead, I'm pep-talking my sisters about crap I barely understand.

In theory, I'm cool with Dayton's lifestyle because he always seems scary to me. I've seen him scare people without doing much. I figured his reputation meant he was a badass, so I didn't need to worry about the details.

"Can I have some?" I ask Ruby.

"Get a spoon and dig in."

My sisters and I eat ice cream and watch the kids. The conversation remains dead until our men arrive home in a burst of activity.

Camden is in a bitch of a mood and throws Daisy over his shoulder before hauling her back to their place.

Bonn stands very still while staring at me as if willing me to get the hell out.

Dayton struts into the condo and tells Keanu how Carl needs to go next door to our place.

After hugging Ruby, I take Keanu's hand and follow Dayton, who doesn't have a care in the world.

Keanu runs to his room to get Carl's truck and then runs back into the living room to play. Dayton and I watch the boy disappear. Once he's gone, we begin to speak but shut up as soon as he reappears. Realizing privacy is a luxury of the childless, I word my question carefully.

"What happens now?"

"About what?" Dayton mumbles before kissing away my reply.

His lips don't leave mine until Keanu's explosion noises draw us apart.

"About the person who did that thing today," I finally ask.

"How would I know?"

"Not only do I think you know who did it, but I also bet you have an idea what needs to be done."

"You think that, huh?" Dayton asks, smirking.

"Yes, I do." I wrap my arms around his waist. "I think you've known what you need to do for a while. However, you don't want to because a part of you likes the guy. Or feels sorry for him, at least."

"I don't think I pity the fucker."

"I think you do. You're softer inside than you let on. JJ had a tough upbringing, and he got screwed like Bonn did. Maybe even worse."

Dayton rolls his eyes, but I continue anyway.

"JJ didn't have friends like you and Camden. He didn't meet someone like Ruby. He grew up to be the worst part of Howler. Petty and jealous, he'll burn down everything Bonn has, but it won't be enough. Next, he'll think Camden has life too easy. Then, he'll turn on you. Eventually, he'll turn on everyone because the feeling he craves is something he'll never find."

"That's a great read on someone you've met only in passing."

Still hugging him, I wish I felt as confident as my words imply. "I know people who can't find satisfaction. Nothing makes them happy. Those people always self-destruct. Those like JJ will drag down others, too."

"So, I finish him before he finishes me?"

Dayton holds my gaze, daring me to give him permission to kill a man.

"JJ thinks you're his friend. He trusts you. For now, you're safe. However, the people you care about aren't. And if JJ ever ends up in jail, he'll bring down the entire club."

"You want me to do it."

My heart hates to continue this conversation. I don't want Dayton to do ugly things. He should live a pampered, safe life where ugly things happen to other people.

My brain tells me to keep talking, though. After all, Dayton's pampered life is anything but safe.

181

"I want someone to do it," I admit. "But I don't trust your father or Howler to make the call until it's too late."

"And Camden?"

"He couldn't get close enough to JJ to make it look like an OD or suicide."

Dayton snorts. "Where did you come up with those ideas?"

"I watch TV, Dayton. I don't know how things work, but I know you do. When JJ's friend attacked Daisy and Ruby, the jerk didn't move away like people said. More likely, he stopped breathing. There are rules in Hickory Creek, and he broke them."

"Mojo did make clear to the club how Bonn wasn't to be harmed until approved by him. Of course, JJ could claim he isn't a member of the club yet."

"If the cops busted him and he turned on the club, do you think your dad would blow off the betrayal as a technicality?"

"You really want him gone," he says, making me feel like a monster.

"JJ is a threat to the people who matter most to me," I say and glance at Keanu. "I sound like a devious bitch, but that man scares me. Of course, I'm unable to do anything more than talk big."

"Don't cry," he says as I blink away tears. "I can't have you crying. Then, Keanu will cry. Soon, I'll cry. You seriously don't want to see me bawling like a baby."

"I could handle it," I say, hugging him tighter. "I'm tough for the people I love."

"I know you are."

"So are you."

Dayton studies my face for the longest minute of my life. Finally, he says, "I'll handle things."

Swallowing hard, I feel like shit to even have this conversation. However, I'll live with the guilt.

"Even if you don't," I say, stroking Dayton's chest, "I'll still think you're the best."

"Even better than Keanu?"

I frown up at him. "Why would you ask a question with an answer that'll make you cry?"

"I thought you were okay with me crying."

"Yeah, but I don't think you'll enjoy it. I get headaches when I cry. After Anita died, I walked around with a stuffed-up nose and a headache. Wasn't fun."

"Let's make a deal for tonight. We don't talk about my business or yours," he says, caressing the scratches on my arms from Millie. "We'll order delivery and hang out here and pretend nothing exists outside this condo."

I glance around Dayton's arm to make sure Keanu is still focused on his toys. Seeing my boy's attention elsewhere, I smile at my sexy man.

"I miss making out with you back at the Red Barn. You'd come in, and we'd talk and flirt and make out. Let's do that tonight once Keanu's asleep. Just make out without any sex."

"Has my dick wronged you in some way?" he asks, leaning away from me. "Why else would you punish the damn thing after all the love it's gifted you?"

Laughing, I run my hand between his legs and give his dick a gentle squeeze.

"We'll have sex later. When we kiss on the couch, I want to pretend it won't go anywhere. Let a girl have her fantasy, will ya?"

"What's so sexy about that fantasy?"

Thinking back to my crush on Dayton, I can't believe how young and silly I'd been.

"Roleplaying is fun. I want to be the old Harmony who never dreamed she could keep you. Then, I can return to reality, where I'm the luckiest gal around. Is that so wrong?"

"Oh, sweet Harmony, you are so into me. It's pretty sad, really," he teases, backing away and heading for the couch where Keanu joins us. "Your mom likes me, kid."

Keanu smiles at me. "Mom likes me, too."

"Yes, I love my boys," I say, messing with their hair.

"We're ordering in," Dayton tells Keanu. "What does Carl want to eat?"

My son whispers to his toy, all while grinning at Dayton. My guys are getting pretty attached to each other. Keanu even chooses to sit next to Dayton when we have dinner later.

Once my mind stops obsessing over JJ taking a shot at Bonn, I'm the happiest I've ever been. Eventually, reality returns, making me worry about Dayton's next move. I say nothing to him, though. He's a man who does his plotting solo.

FORTY-FIVE — DAYTON

I doubt JJ felt the shot to the head.

The roofie I slipped in his beer knocked him out. Then, I maneuvered his gun in his hand, leveled it against his head, and helped him pull the trigger.

A good investigator might question the scene, but we don't have those around Hickory Creek Township. If it looks like a suicide, the cops rule it as one.

My dad visits me the day after Howler finds JJ dead. While Harmony is at work and Keanu's at daycare, Mojo comes by the condo. Even knowing we're alone, he checks out the bedrooms.

"Paranoid?" I ask him.

"Did you hear about JJ?"

"Is that a real question? Everyone's heard about it. He was Howler's son and under the club's protection. His death is big news."

Mojo studies my face. "Rumor has it that he killed himself."

"JJ was a complicated guy."

"I wouldn't know. He never had much interest in spending time with me."

"You sound real broken up about that," I say and yawn.

"He was a squirrelly fucker. I've never seen the point of wasting time getting to know one of the millions of Howler's bastards."

"Yet, you would have let him in the club if he jumped through enough hoops."

"That's the theory anyway."

My dad falls silent and takes a seat at one of the kitchen stools. I use the silence to think back to JJ's expression when he opened the door for me. He was clearly waiting to see if I'd accuse him of taking a shot at Bonn. *That's when I knew he did it.*

I hadn't accused him, of course. We enjoyed a beer and talked about those hoops the club expected him to jump through.

I wouldn't be surprised if JJ knew deep down how Howler would never come through in the end. When his father eventually did him wrong, JJ had two choices—let it go or fuck up everything Howler cared about. *Not a tough decision for a man like him.*

Dad taps his fingers on the kitchen island and says, "I was around twenty the first time I killed someone I knew. We weren't tight, but I'd seen him grow up. His name was Ryan, and I beat his head in with a tire iron. He wasn't the first guy I killed, but his death messed me up a little. It felt too personal."

"Why are you telling me this?"

"You know why," Mojo says, holding my gaze.

"What I know is I'll do what needs to be done to protect my family and the club. Is that what you're talking about?"

"I guess it is."

"Since we're having a heart-to-heart, let me ask you something. Are you ever planning on retiring? Or will you make Camden wait until he's an old man?"

"Just spitting that out without a care in the world, are you, boy?"

"It's what everyone is thinking, but no one has the balls to ask. My testicles feel fine, so let's put things out on the table."

Dad doesn't answer immediately. When he does, he dodges the heart of the matter. "Howler isn't ready to step down."

"I didn't ask about him."

"As a man, I'd stick around until my last fucking breath. I got no interest in walking away. As a father, I should give you boys your time to rule. As the Brotherhood's president, I know it's a young man's game. I've felt that clock ticking since Kirk Johansson handed over the Reapers to his kid. The expectation from Memphis is that my turn to step aside is coming soon."

Tapping my fingers on the counter, I hadn't expected him to be so honest. I take a minute to get my thoughts in order.

"If you go out now, you look strong," I finally say. "If you wait until you're pressured out, you'll look like an old man grasping for his former glory."

"What will I do with myself if I'm not running the Brotherhood?"

"Run other shit, I guess. Maybe Mom will give you a job."

"Funny, asshole," he grumbles and tosses one of Keanu's LEGOs at me.

"Or you could be the guy that makes deals for the club. The ambassador to Memphis or something. Still around but handing over the day-to-day to Camden. It's what I'd do if I were you."

"Is it?"

"Yeah. I don't want to spend my entire life doing the same shit. When my kids get grown-up, I plan to figure out something to keep Harmony and me entertained until we're dead."

"So, that girl's the real deal, huh?"

"Well, yeah, that's why I mentioned Harmony and me being together until we're dead."

"And you're cool with another man's kid?"

Sighing, I'm so fucking sick of people pointing out how Keanu's not my biological son.

"Harmony is my woman, and that makes him my kid. Blood doesn't mean shit. If it did, JJ might be alive and well."

"Fair enough."

"Don't blow shit off," I mutter. "This thing with Harmony will last. That means you'll treat her with respect. The kid, too. Not because you're my president, but because you're my father. If you don't respect them, then don't expect to be invited to family get-togethers."

"Watch your threats, Dayton," he warns, glaring at me.

"If you weren't willing to threaten your father over Mom and your kids, then you aren't much of a man. I'm just doing what you'd do."

"Fine, but don't be surprised if the kid grows up to resent you for not being his real dad."

"Every kid grows up to resent his parents," I say, holding his gaze.

"I did right by you."

"Yeah, you did. *In the past.* Of course, how you treat my woman and kid isn't in the past."

"Got it," he says, standing up. "Once Howler gets over his self-pity about JJ, I'll talk to him about changing club leadership. The Brotherhood needs a fresh look, and everyone knows who should take over."

"Yes, they do."

I show him to the door, where he pauses. "I'm glad things are working for you, Dayton. People were beginning to think you'd turn into a fucking lush."

"Yeah, people tend to think what I want them to think. Good to know my bullshit fooled them."

Dad grins and gives my shoulder a hard pat. "Tell your woman to invite me over sometime for dinner. I'll play grandpa to the kid."

Watching him walk down the hall, I get a weird heat in my gut. Fuck me, if I don't want to crawl into my room and hide away until Harmony and Keanu return home.

I killed JJ without blinking an eye. I stood up to my dad and got a little fatherly pride in return. Another badass would let that shit roll off him. He might down a few beers and drown his emotions. Hell, he might take a long ride to clear his thoughts.

What I need is for Harmony to say she loves me and then Keanu to tell me about his day with Carl. I need soft and safe. After all, outside of this condo, the world doesn't offer much comfort, even for a spoiled fuck like me.

FORTY-SIX — HARMONY

For the last few days, JJ's suicide is all anyone in Hickory Creek Township can talk about. Conspiracies abound, but the preferred one is that someone from out of town came to settle a debt. I never offer my view when anyone asks. My mouth remains tightly shut because I don't trust myself not to sound relieved by JJ's death.

The one person who doesn't gossip about it is Dayton. He never mentions his cousin's name. Dayton puts on his stoned expression when anyone around us brings up the topic. This trick prevents people from expecting him to contribute to the conversation.

Dayton seems unaffected by what he did to JJ until the night I arrive home to the condo with Keanu after work. At first, I assume the place is empty, though I saw his Harley parked in the garage.

"Where's Day?" Keanu asks me.

I smile at how he's shortened Dayton's name. No doubt, he thinks it sounds close to what Elle calls her father.

"I don't know. Is he taking a nap?"

Keanu runs to the master bedroom and peeks inside. He shakes his head and runs into the room to check the bathroom. The little guy races out.

"In my room?" he asks Carl while barreling toward second bedroom.

I grin at how Keanu now understands the room belongs to him, and we're going to live here. He's still a little confused by how he won't live in the trailer anymore once our boxes come over.

Appearing from the bedroom, Keanu has a helicopter in his free hand. He's been in love with the toy since Dayton bought it at the store. The thing cost less than five bucks, but Keanu is so protective of the toy that he won't even let Elle hold it.

"He's not here," Keanu says, looking confused.

"Maybe he went to someone's condo. He'll come home soon."

A disappointed Keanu sighs. He waits all day to see Dayton since the hunk can't get his ass out of bed before ten.

While I check the pot roast I started this morning, Keanu goes to the balcony door. He knows there's a special lock Dayton installed so our boy can't get outside unsupervised. Looking through the door, Keanu jumps up and down.

"Day!" he yells, tapping on the door.

I see a hand reach out and tug the slider open. Keanu hurries outside, and I hear him telling Dayton how we couldn't find him.

Walking to the balcony, I am a little nervous about what kind of mood Dayton might be in. Or if he's been drinking all day.

"Hey," I say softly, coming out to where he sits in a chair with Keanu on his lap.

Dayton's expression reveals nothing. He takes my hand and tugs me closer. Per the routine, he checks my arms for new scratches. Finding none, he nods.

"Good day?" Dayton asks.

"Yeah, it was. Are you okay?"

Even nodding, Dayton avoids my gaze and focuses on Keanu, who tells him how he ate fish sticks for lunch. I watch them smile at each other, both seeming in a good mood. Of course, Keanu isn't faking his smile.

Dayton remains too quiet for the rest of the evening. No suggestive comments to me. He doesn't even cop a feel when Keanu isn't looking.

By the time our little guy is tired and ready to climb in bed, Dayton seems prepared to do the same. He rests in a chair, watching Keanu fall asleep. I stand at the door, watching them both.

I don't know what to do with a depressed Dayton, assuming that's the emotion he's feeling. I'm used to him being angry, cocky, hungover, and even silly. This silent routine is new.

Climbing into his lap, I kiss him gently. "Keanu loves you so much," I whisper. "Almost as much as me."

"It's not a competition," Dayton murmurs, fighting a grin.

"If it were, I'd kick his little butt."

Dayton finally smiles. "My dad came by today to give me a pat on the back for dealing with JJ."

"And his approval made you feel like a dick."

"I am a dick."

"But not like how he is."

"No, I'm a different breed," he says, leaning his head back on the wall. "He wanted me to know it's okay to feel bad about doing what I did."

"It's okay to feel any damn thing you want," I whisper and nuzzle his throat. "No one owns your feelings, and they don't have to make sense."

Dayton wraps his arms around me. "From the moment JJ walked into my life, I knew how he'd leave. Is that the kind of man you want around your boy?"

"I always knew you were a bad man, Dayton. What I've learned these last few weeks is how you're much more than your reputation. You're sweet and funny and loyal and romantic and capable of loving in a way I never thought anyone would love me. The fact that you also adore Keanu makes you better than even my wildest fantasy."

Dayton smiles at me, and I spot his usual confidence in his rich brown eyes. Even in the dark room with only the ocean nightlight illuminating his face, I know he's shaking loose of the melancholy he felt all evening.

"It was a Thursday when I saw you with Keanu," he whispers while his fingers tease the back of my neck. "That's when I decided to lock down my dick and wait for you. You were wearing a tie-dye skirt and a Bananarama shirt. I remember because I had to look up what the fuck Bananarama meant."

Giggling, I press my mouth against his shoulder to keep from waking Keanu.

"You were so beautiful, and I saw how much you loved that kid. Shit, the look on your face alone was amazing enough for me to wait for you."

"I'm glad you did, stud."

Dayton's fingers slide down my back and wrap possessively around my hip.

"That outfit you wore back then wouldn't be good for camping."

"What?"

Dayton grunts and nips at my ear. "I lost my tribe," he growls. "I'm all alone in the woods. I need to breed."

Laughing, I cover my mouth while he stands in an easy motion. Once we're out of Keanu's bedroom, I pretend to pound on Dayton's chest.

"Let me down, you beast."

Dayton only growls, having regressed into full Big Foot mode. He doesn't find his words until after he's nearly chewed off my panties and bred a little beast into my womb.

For a bad man, he sure knows how to pamper a woman.

FORTY-SEVEN — DAYTON

Bonn and Ruby's wedding is a small affair with twenty people attending. Neither of them is decked out in anything fancy. Ruby wears a pale red dress. Bonn sports slacks and a buttoned-up shirt but no tie. This is the kind of wedding I can respect—no pompous flare bullshit.

The real fun happens at the Boogie Bowl for the reception. The Slater girls love their 1980s crap music. Bonn's a fan, too. They joyfully dance to bands long irrelevant. Harmony insists I join Keanu and her on the dance floor.

"I love this song," Harmony says, bouncing around while holding a jumping Keanu's hands.

I shuffle my feet to the sugary sweet pop song. "Is a girl singing?"

"No, it's Depeche Mode," she laughs and gives Ruby an amused smile.

"You've never heard 'Just Can't Get Enough' before?" Ruby asks me.

"I listen to good music, Ruby. I'm sorry if that poops on your wedding bliss, but I refuse to lie."

Harmony and Ruby laugh at me, but I'm too busy enjoying how high Keanu's jumps get. The kid has some serious spring in his step. Maybe his dad was part cat.

Eventually, both of my parents get into the dancing mood. Though not with each other. Mom and Erik slow dance to an overwrought song while Dad feels up a broad he met at the grocery store.

A dozen times, Camden tries to talk to me. I have zero interest in discussing the upcoming super-duper important club meeting. We both know what's going to happen. Everyone does. No one is even pretending it's a secret. Hell, for over a week, Howler's been crying in his beer like a guy about to be laid off.

Avoiding Camden, I enjoy a beaming Harmony in her pink outfit and Keanu in his dinosaur shirt. Every time someone points out what he's wearing, he roars.

"I taught him that," I tell Harmony. "Nothing scares the peasants like a roaring beast."

Holding my gaze, she gives me a sly smile. "Don't I know it."

This woman drives me fucking crazy with her knowing looks. I'd take her somewhere private if not for the kid and how her sisters expect Harmony to stick around for a few karaoke numbers.

By the time the Slater girls drunkenly sing, "Do You Really Want to Hurt Me," Keanu is zonked out on my lap, and Elle looks ready to do the same in Bonn's.

Earlier in the evening, my cousin thanked me for the help. Those are the only words we'll exchange about JJ. He knows I have his back, so we can skip the sappy sentiments.

"Look at us whipped family men," Camden says, holding Daisy's purse.

"Pink is a good color on you," I tell him.

We share a smile before maneuvering our drunken women to the SUVs outside. Elle gets a ride home with Harmony and me so her parents can start a mini-honeymoon.

Even sloppy drunk, Harmony manages to tuck in the kids, ride me into submission, and get up by six for work. That's my woman. She'll work a Saturday shift to help Millie to her doctor's appointment. I used to think her job was a problem. Now, I get how it makes her feel like a badass in the same way my club does for me.

With Harmony at work, I'm in charge of Keanu and Elle for the morning. Daisy offers to help, but I don't want Camden thinking I can't handle two small people under my care. The man already gets to be the top dog in our club. No way am I giving him anything more to brag about.

I end up taking the kids out for breakfast, thinking it'll be easier than cooking for them. Except children can't eat without dumping half of their meals on their clothes.

"I made a mess," Keanu says, looking down at where the syrup-covered pancake attached itself to his shirt.

"Shit happens."

"Shit happens," he tells Carl.

"Don't say shit," Elle tells Keanu.

"Shit," Keanu immediately says.

I remove the food from his clothes before leaning down to make eye contact with the little man.

"Shit is a grown-up word. Is Carl grown-up?"

Keanu looks at his toy and shakes his head.

"Well, then he can't say shit."

Keanu nods and reaches for his milk, knocking it over. Fortunately, the thing has a lid on the top.

"Are you this messy at home?" I ask.

Giving me one of his double shoulder shrugs, the kid makes another attempt with his pancakes. He drops more food and knocks over his drink three more times before I notice how a lady nearby has one of those booster seats for her kid.

"I blame you," I tell Elle once Keanu sits up higher and stops dropping everything. "You should have told me he needed one."

"I'm not his mom."

"Neither am I."

"You're his dad," she says, chewing her sausage link. "You should know."

Keanu doesn't react to her dad comment. He's too busy working a fork with one hand and keeping Carl snugly in the other.

When they're done making a mess, I know where I want to take them next. We stop by a pet store near the condo.

"Kittens," Elle coos.

"Fish!" Keanu announces, seeing the pictures on the front window.

"I want to get an aquarium for the condo," I tell Keanu while unbuckling him from his car seat. "That way, you can look at fish at home."

Keanu doesn't get what I'm saying. He just wants to see the fish. I ask him to help me pick out the ones he wants, but he decides to name all of them instead.

"Fish are ugly," Elle whispers to me while Keanu stares at them in awe. "They have ugly eyes."

"You Slater women always want cats. However, men like Keanu and me want something less high maintenance."

Elle stares at me the way Keanu does when I say something he doesn't understand.

"Can I look at the kittens?"

Agreeing, I end up standing halfway between both kids to keep an eye on them. I also manage to talk to a woman about what I'd need for a good-sized aquarium in my house.

Since the move, Keanu cries whenever he thinks he can't go back to his trailer. I hope an aquarium at the condo will finally convince him to let go of the tiny home he's known for the first few years of his life.

Despite what Harmony thinks, sometimes, I can buy my way out of a problem. Wooing a kid with a big purchase is what my mom would do, and I'm nothing if not a mama's boy.

EPILOGUE — HARMONY

Dayton and I make a deal regarding a second child. We won't consider another kid until my IUD needs replacing. That gives us two solid years of enjoying life as a threesome.

We spend the time eating out a lot. Dayton takes Keanu to the zoo a few times a month, and we drive down to Florida to visit LEGOLAND. For several years, we enjoy a relaxed lifestyle.

I love my job at the group home, especially watching my clients leave adolescence and become women. They're like a second family to me. I care for them during the day and focus on my guys in the evenings and weekends.

Once Mojo and Howler embrace retirement, Camden and Dayton step into leadership roles. Even with more responsibilities, Dayton still picks up Keanu every day from daycare. The club is his second family, but Keanu and I always come first.

Though a baby isn't on our to-do list, my sisters have other plans. Less than a year after getting married, Ruby gives birth to her baby boy, Adric.

Meanwhile, Daisy and Camden start their family with Lincoln. Soon, they're looking for a bigger place. Dayton claims we ought to stay at the condo just to spite them.

Well, just until he hears someone say how lucky Camden's kids are to have a yard. Oh, yeah, now we need a house, too.

I convince Dayton to stay in the condo for as long as possible. I'm not a fan of suburbia and figure we won't fit in with our neighbors. I'm trailer trash. Keanu doesn't look like everyone else. Dayton is a jerk who refuses to edit himself. We don't need to live next to judgmental people when we have a perfectly nice home.

Dayton bends to my will for nearly a year after our baby comes along.

Calypso "Soso" Anita Rutgers is a chill baby. She sleeps a lot and rarely cries. Eventually, she learns to laugh whenever she burps and farts. She's Dayton with a bow in her blonde hair.

Blame my reasoning on pregnancy hormones, but I choose the name Calypso to annoy my mom and Dayton's.

Sally says more than once, "It's a name for a hippy's child. I thought you weren't a hippy."

"My daughter, Calypso, won't judge me for being a hippy," I announce.

Though Clara doesn't mention my name choice, she does wear a frozen smile whenever I use it. Feeling stubborn, I refuse to back down.

Dayton is no help. He's so mad once he learns we're expecting a girl that he refuses to participate in naming her. Getting my way, I put Calypso on her birth certificate. Then, within days, I decide I don't like the name and won't use it.

In the end, Calypso gets shortened to Soso, which is a Native American name for "Tree Squirrel Dining on Pine Nuts." *Talk about embracing my inner hippy.*

Dayton gets over his resentment about having a girl as soon as he holds Soso. He stares in awe at her, telling anyone who will listen how she's the best-looking baby in history. He's crazy about her. In fact, I'm forced to throw a few fits just so he'll share her.

I take a year off from the group home to stay with Soso, only picking up occasional weekend shifts to give me time out of the house. I'm happy to take Keanu to school every day for his first year. He is so excited about school, even if it means leaving behind Carl and Soso.

By Halloween, he hates class and cries every morning when we get ready.

"Homeschool him," Clara says one day. "Hudson didn't do well at school. Some kids just don't fit into the school mold."

"I planned to go back to work, and I don't know how to teach Keanu."

"I'll hire someone to organize his studies. I promise we'll figure it out so Keanu learns in a better environment."

Ruby tells me Hayes's kids are homeschooled, and Elle wants to be, too. The idea doesn't seem so wild, and I hate how miserable Keanu is on school days.

"Fuck school," is Dayton's response when we talk about the situation. "Half of the crap he'll learn he won't need. The other half isn't that damn complicated. Let him learn at home if that's what makes him happy."

"I worry I'll make the wrong decision, and he'll resent me for not making him go. Like he'll miss out on stuff."

A baby-wearing Dayton wraps an arm around my shoulders. "Keanu is my son. That makes him special, meaning he deserves special treatment."

"Can't argue with that logic."

"No, you really can't."

This is the Dayton I didn't know existed all those years when I crushed on him. The fiercely protective man refuses to see his loved ones suffer. He'll never wear a "#1 Dad" shirt, but he's the kind of father I could only dream of growing up and then for Keanu.

I was wrong about Dayton. He *is* complicated. My husband is good and bad, all rolled into a perfect package. He's both an insider with wealth and power and an outsider never quite on the same page as those in his family and club. As complex as he can be, I've never once regretted loving him. I never will.

EPILOGUE — DAYTON

People always claim Camden took to fatherhood easily. I let that crap go most days. However, I occasionally point out how I'm the natural fucking father between the two of us. Sure, Camden digs his kids who look like him and have his blood running through his veins. It's natural to love what you've created. Camden is doing what's easy.

I'm the father of a child who doesn't look like me, but I love him like he's my own. That's not natural. Like JJ said, in the animal kingdom, males don't normally take non-biological offspring under their wings.

I did it, though. *On account of being a natural father.* Like Camden, I'd kill and die for my kids. No one messes with Keanu without suffering my wrath. He's my boy, and he knows it, too. I'm even learning Korean, which is no easy feat. I want to be ready for our trip to meet Ji-Hoon's family once the kids are old enough to handle the flight.

The only area I'll admit Camden beats me is with his kids' names. Harmony truly has no gift for naming children. Since it's her only flaw, I don't obsess over it.

Our daughter looks just like Harmony. Soso's big brown eyes are the only physical feature she gets from me. She's a gorgeous little person who smells and cries and excels at the usual baby horrors. Yet, I don't mind any of it. She's mine and perfect. I want to hold her as much as possible before she grows up and finds a man to steal her away.

I was admittedly pissed when I found out we were having a girl. Not because I wanted a son as much as I didn't want a daughter. Pink, dolls, and more pink are not things I can find common ground with like Keanu and I did with fish and LEGOs. I had no sisters, no chick friends, and I'm not built to be a father to a daughter.

Except Soso is as irresistible as her mother. Completely in awe of her, I don't care if my daughter spends her life talking about unicorns and tampons. I won't be able to deny her a damn thing.

Funny how having a wife and kids makes a man focus on the future. Harmony and I get married on the way to Florida's LEGOLAND. We sign the papers, say I do in an office, and then move on with our trip. Nothing fancy is necessary. She's been mine for as long as I can remember. The paperwork is just a formality.

Camden has big plans for moving the club toward Nashville. He wants more chapters, more territory, more everything. Sounds great, but once his kids come along, his plans slow down.

I'm glad for a lazier pace. Hickory Creek is my town, and I want to remain here. It's where my woman works, my kids play, and my parents live. I don't crave one-upping my father's legacy like Camden does. I just want to pay the bills and keep my club brothers happy. Anything more feels greedy.

Or maybe fatherhood steals my balls. After all, I'd rather spend my afternoons with Keanu, talking about fish, Harleys, and Carl's scarred-up face than beating down a dealer or a pimp in a town that doesn't mean shit to me.

The kid gets me, and I understand him. As a twin, I shared everything in life.

I'm number one with Harmony, Keanu, and eventually, Soso. I don't need to share, and they never view me as a second choice. I've always seen myself as the better twin. Now, I'm surrounded by people cool enough to see me the same way.

Nearly losing out on having them in my life still pisses me off. One night, I bailed on Harmony and pissed away my future. Regret almost ate me alive, leaving booze as my only escape. Until I finally stopped obsessing over what I fucked up and started focusing on what I needed to do to win over my woman and her little man.

THE END

Printed in Dunstable, United Kingdom

66773821R00116